THE GUNS OF PALEMBANG

Other books in this series
available from New English Library:

SPOILS OF WAR
THE FIRST BLOOD
THE DEADLIEST GAME
AMBUSH AT DERATI WELLS

THE GUNS OF PALEMBANG

Peter McCurtin

NEW ENGLISH LIBRARY/TIMES MIRROR

First published in the USA by
Tower Publications, Inc in 1977

First NEL paperback edition August 1978

NEL Books are published by
New English Library Limited from
Barnard's Inn, Holborn,
London EC1N 2JR
Made and printed in Great Britain by
Hunt Barnard Printing Ltd,
Aylesbury, Bucks

45003869 6

One

Never get drunk in a city you don't know.

That was a rule I had learned the hard way a long time back, but had temporarily forgotten. It can be very dangerous to booze heavily in a strange place, particularly in the Orient. You make yourself fair game for all the dagger-wielding muggers and doped-up thieves that a primitive city can breed. You become a potential victim.

Not that I had gotten all that drunk, on that hot, sultry night in Bangkok. I had left the hotel primarily to get a whiff of breathable air, and to pick up some Sketolene for the dive-bombing mosquitoes in my room, and the other exotic fauna there. The big chinchuk lizards on my walls – the kind that send lady tourists at the Rama Hotel into immediate and high-decibel hysterics – had not done their job, and I was being pestered to death.

On the way to the store, though, I had found a nice little bar, sitting on the edge of a muddy-water canal called a *klong* by the locals. The place had had big ceiling fans and a high grade bourbon, so I had stayed longer than I should have, and was feeling the liquor some when I left. I had given up on the Sketolene by that time, calculating that the alcohol was a better defense against the ravages of humming and crawling insects.

There was an old beat-up taxi sitting across the narrow street when I emerged from the bar, and I walked over to it blithely. It was not until I had leaned down to speak with the driver that I saw that he already had a fellow sitting beside him, up front in the vehicle.

'Oh,' I said sluggishly. 'I thought you were free.'

'Yes, free. I take you,' the driver encouraged me. He had a hard-looking face with a mottled complexion, and he was a rather brawny fellow. 'This here is friend. I take him home after you. You get in, mister.'

I gave the other fellow a glance, and nodded. If I had been dead sober, I would have been more cautious. But in my mellow mood brought on by the bourbon, I did not think twice about riding away in a taxi with two men.

'Right,' I said, climbing into the rear seat.

My hotel – a two-bit place called the Thai – was across town. The taxi went slowly, crossing the dark canals and occasionally passing an ancient green-and-gold temple. When we passed the Temple of the Reclining Buddah, I realized we were heading in the wrong direction. I sat up in the back seat, and looked around.

'Hey,' I said.

The driver did not turn. 'Yes?' he said curtly.

'We're going the wrong damned way,' I protested.

'It's okay, mister. I take my friend where he go first. Everything okay.'

The friend turned and looked at me, and I saw that his face was even harder than the driver's. It was narrow and long, with slitted eyes and a ramrod chin. He grinned an ugly grin at me.

'That's swell of you,' I said to the driver. 'But I thought you were heading to the hotel first.'

'It's faster this way,' the driver assured me. 'You sit back, mister. Everything okay.'

His voice now told me that he did not much care what I thought of his explanation. I looked out onto the street and saw that we were headed out of town. We were already on a small back street on our way out of the city.

'Faster, hell,' I muttered. 'I don't know where the hell you're going, but you can pull over and let me out right here. I'll get another cab.'

The driver grunted, and kept going. The houses and buildings were getting sparse along the road, and I saw the hulk of a water buffalo in a nearby field.

'Hey, damn it!' I said loudly. 'Pull over!'

The driver ignored me completely now. The fellow with the slitted eyes beside him turned again to look at me. 'In just a moment,' he said casually, not grinning any more.

My eyes held his gaze, and I wondered what was behind that

hard stare. But I was beginning to get an idea, even in my altered state. Before I could protest further, though, the car pulled off the street and up beside a low building that looked deserted.

We were in a remote area now. The nearest other building was a hundred yards away, and directly across the road we had turned off were open fields, part of a small farm.

'All right, mister,' the driver told me. 'Now you get out, yes?'

I regarded their hard faces somberly, then opened my door and climbed out beside the building. The long-faced man followed me out of the cab, and the driver cut the engine.

I had sobered up enough to know I was in big trouble.

I saw the short length of pipe in the right hand of Long-face now, and as the driver got out and came around the front of the taxi, I could see a kind of black-jack in his stubby fist. He was even heftier than he had looked in the car, and had a fat belly that hung over his trousers waist.

Fat-belly grinned at me pleasantly, and showed me the black-jack. 'You will pay the fare now,' he suggested.

Suddenly I was sobering up fast. I wished I had brought my Star .45 from the hotel, the stubby automatic I usually carried with me. But who takes a gun to buy Sketolene?

'And how much would that be?' I asked the driver with the belly.

The other man, Long-face, grinned harshly again. 'Everything you have, Yankee,' he said in good English.

If I had had a good-sized bank roll on me, the whole incident might have ended uneventfully at that point. But I had spent almost all of my Thai *baht* on the bourbon, and had very little to offer them.

I pulled the few pieces of dirty paper money from my pocket, and proffered them. 'That's all there is,' I said. 'If you want more, sue me.'

Fat-belly's face sagged into straight lines, and Long-face looked very angry. 'You lie, Yankee. Give it all to us, or we begin on you.'

'Go to hell,' I told him. I threw the *baht* on the ground at their feet. 'That's my burnt offering. Take it or leave it.'

That did not endear me to Long-face. He came at me surprisingly fast, swinging the length of pipe. I swore under my breath, raising my arm in defense, but sluggishly because of the liquor. The pipe thudded against my forearm, face and head. I felt explosive pain in all three places, and saw fireworks go off in the front of my skull, and then I was hitting the ground on my back.

I lay there gasping for a moment, then tried to rise. I got half-way up, and Fat-belly swung the black-jack and connected with my neck and head. The pain exploded again, and I went down again. I could hear some swearing and muttering between them, and some hands going through my pockets.

'There isn't any more money.'

'They always carry money. He must have it hidden.'

They really went at it then. They tore my suit to shreds, looking in the lining and cuffs and other places. They pulled it off me brutally, then wrenched my shoes off without untying the laces, and examined them at length. I was just recovering enough to try to defend myself again, when they gave it up and turned on me angrily.

'You cheat us, heh?' the Fat-belly growled. He kicked me in the back, alongside the spine.

I yelled out in new pain.

'You filthy dog! You don't get away with this!' Long-face yelled at me. He kicked out savagely at my leg. He just missed destroying my kneecap as the blow glanced off my leg just above the knee.

Fat-belly now came again from his side, aiming a kick at my head. I threw up my hands and tried to block the blow, and it thudded against my arms but still caught me at the base of the skull. A nausea welled up in my insides, and a blackness crept up around the edges of my consciousness.

The other man, Long-face, now kicked out again at me, connecting in my anterior ribs and snapping one loudly. I yelled aloud. He kicked again, expertly, like a Thai boxer, and the hard shoe thumped up under the ribs, in soft flesh there. I grunted hard and the blackness welled up again. I felt a hard kick to my back, and that did it. The blackness swirled in like muddy water in a local canal, and then I seemed to be falling down a long incline, tumbling head over heels toward a swampy, murky place below.

I haven't been in many hospitals in my life, but those two bastards put me in the local one for several days. I wound up with severe concussion, a slightly fractured cheekbone, and two cracked ribs. That was in addition to several bad cuts, and bruises all over my head and body. They had worked me over good. They had done a job on me. And all because I had not had enough money on me to satisfy their greed.

I determined never to walk the streets of Bangkok alone at night again. I decided to keep my drinks to one, in places like that local bar, too. And lastly, I resolved that if I ran into my two playmates again before I left the city, I would return the favor they had bestowed on me.

The police, of course, had tried to help. But I did not have the number of the taxi. I did not even know for certain that it really was a taxi. And my description of my two assailants was so general, they told me, as to be useless. But I knew I would know those men if I ever saw them again.

I had been planning to leave Bangkok the day after the assault, but the hospitalization delayed me. I had been in town to deliver a prototype military revolver to the Thai army. I had distribution rights for a South American manufacturer. I had made a small deal and was ready to fly to Macao on other business.

But that delay in the hospital changed all that. An Indonesian military man, who had flown all the way from Djakarta to see me and who would have missed me if I had left when I planned, caught me at the hospital on my last evening there.

'I am pleased to meet you, Jim Rainey,' he said to me, as he stood very straight and tall at the side of my bed, shaking my hand in his sturdy, tanned one. 'Your reputation precedes you.'

'My pleasure, General Surabaya,' I told him. 'Sorry to meet with you under these circumstances. But a couple of eager locals gave me a royal Thai welcome the other night.'

He grinned. He was a rather big man, wearing a khaki uniform with several impressive-looking medals strung across the front. He had a broad Indonesian face and a perpetual set to his mouth that could have been a hard smile or an expression of pained impatience with the world.

'I hope you are not seriously injured?' he asked, with a suddenly proprietary interest.

'Just minor things,' I said. 'What brings you all the way to Bangkok just to speak with me, General?'

Surabaya sighed heavily and took a seat beside the bed. 'I suppose you know all the trouble my poor country has had in recent years,' he said, 'with political upheavals of one kind or another.'

I nodded. 'I know what a time the Commies have given you,' I said. 'Particularly in '65 and '68.'

'Yes, the 1968 uprising almost succeeded,' said Surabaya. 'Poor common folk are easily deluded, Rainey. I suppose there will always be a place for ruthless promise-makers in the world, so long as we are unable to substantially raise the standard of living of the common man.'

'Are the Communists at it again down your way?' I asked him.

He nodded in the affirmative. 'There is a newly-formed People's Liberation Army which is completely underground. At first they only broadcast on short-wave radio and bombed an occasional public building, to arouse the baser emotions of the radical leftists in our country. But then they suddenly became ambitious, without our knowing it. A general was murdered, and then a popular rightist colonel. Both men that I knew well, and admired. After that, an anti-Communist Assembly leader met with an unusual accident.'

'An assassination campaign?' I suggested.

'Exactly. We were not sure at first, but then, just a couple of weeks ago, we made a super-secret investigation and burglarized the home of a suspect labor leader named Amir Malik. We found the details of a cold-blooded and ruthless plot to assassinate a dozen top government and military leaders. The names of the three dead men were on the list, and crossed off. Also on the list were myself, our Foreign Minister Dr Asaban, and President Machmud.'

I uttered a low whistle. 'An ambitious undertaking. Do you know who besides Malik is involved?'

'Oh, yes. There are five of them all told, all respected leaders of our society, Rainey, but with known leftist leanings. We were not surprised that Malik would sink so low, but a couple of the names shocked us, I must tell you.'

'So what did you do, arrest them?' I asked.

Surabaya shook his head. 'That did not seem feasible, Rainey. President Machmud did not want to get involved in formal arrests. That might not necessarily stop the plot, you see. When these culprits met in Palembang and planned this ugly thing, they agreed to hire professional killers outside the PLA to do the dirty work with the most efficiency. We do not have the names of these hirelings, who could be directed in the continuation of this plot from behind bars, if we arrested the plotters. Also, if we give these assassins a trial in the courts, things can go wrong. Delays and sob-sister tactics could ruin any chance of quick justice. And in the meantime, they would be able to go on with their plans to murder top officials and replace them with leftists.'

'Also,' I said, 'they may be getting expert supervision from outside.'

'It is possible,' Surabaya agreed. 'There have been Chinese agents in Djakarta in the recent past. We have no real evidence that there is any connection with the outside, but the possibility exists.'

'Well,' I said, 'you have an immediate and urgent problem, General. But I still don't know why you're telling this all to me.'

He grunted. 'Nabi Machmud has had very secret advice from your CIA, Rainey. He rejected it and sent your people away. They wanted to make a political thing of it, use the situation to their advantage. Machmud wants swift counter-action, and nothing else.'

'He wants the plotters dead?' I said.

'Immediately,' Surabaya said, 'if not sooner.' He grinned at his little joke, then the grin faded off his square face. 'Our lives are at stake, Rainey, and our nation's life as well. This ugly plot by terrible people cannot be handled in the usual way. There is no time for polemics or leaning over backwards to be fair with these murderers. There is only stopping them before they succeed.'

'Which means a counter-assassination plot of your own,' I put in.

'Precisely. We want someone who can be trusted to come to Djakarta immediately and supervise a quiet campaign of liquidation of these five murderers, before they manage to liquidate us who came by our leadership jobs legitimately. We think you are the man to do this for us, Rainey.'

I raised my eyebrows slightly. 'I think you've been given some wrong information, General. I'm not a political assassin. I'm a professional soldier. I fight other people's wars for them. I'm a tactician, not a cloak-and-dagger killer.'

'I know your background well, Rainey,' Surabaya assured me. 'In Lebanon, where you recently fought a fight for sanity in their civil strife, you are revered by most, hated by a few, and held in awe by all. You are a legend in your own time, Rainey, from the jungles of Colombia to the back streets of Paris. They still talk of your killing Joe Maltese the assassin – the politicians of Washington, the policemen of Interpol, the suave British DI-5 men. They all know your name, Rainey, and for good reason.'

'They also know the difference between me and Joe Maltese,' I told him. 'At least, I hope they do.'

'Of course they do, and so do we in Djakarta,' Surabaya said quietly. 'We are not trying to make you into a Maltese, Rainey. We want you to go after an organized group of killers, a group that is part of an international army of killers who hope some day to rule the world – the Communist conspiracy. Is this small war that is already under way in Indonesia any less a war because it is carried on secretly? Because the Communists come with their guns in the night, and kill without the fanfare of the battlefield? I don't think so, Rainey. If you are a true professional soldier, I think you will recognize this quiet struggle that lies ahead of us in Djakarta as a kind of military battle, a battle in which the death of one individual is more important than perhaps a thousand deaths on the battlefield.'

I thought about that for a long moment. It had been a great speech, but I had never trusted the words of politicians or generals. They were too good with them. The thing was, though, that these words made a lot of sense.

I looked over at Surabaya. 'The job would be to kill five men?'

'That would be the entire operation. To kill five murderers before they kill the rest of us on their list. Surely there is no moral uncertainty in such an assignment?'

I rubbed my chin, and felt my ribs still hurting. 'Not if I myself were convinced by the evidence against the people I was going after,' I replied slowly. 'Would I be in charge of such an operation?'

'Completely,' Surabaya said. 'You would be given a temporary commission in the Presidential Guard that Machmud recently established – a division of the regular army – and you would be given two hired professionals to work under you. More if you wanted them. No one would know of the operation but you three, me, the President, and the Minister of Foreign Affairs, Dr Asaban.'

The next question was the most important one. 'How much would it pay?' I asked.

Surabaya grinned slightly. 'I was told you would ask that on the first meeting. I like that, Rainey. It shows me you are serious about your work, and about survival. I think you will be pleased with the suggested amount. We are prepared to pay you fifty thousand American dollars for the entire job. That is ten thousand per victim, an attractive figure, I think.'

My jaw must have dropped slightly open. I had never been offered much more than $3,500 per month for soldiering. If a job like this went well, it would all be over in a few weeks, and I would be jingling fifty grand in my pockets. I tried to keep the surprise out of my face.

'Is that the going rate for assassinations?' I asked wryly.

Surabaya laughed in his throat. 'We could buy professional gunmen all through the Pacific and Southeast Asia for five hundred dollars apiece, Rainey. You know that. But we want this project carried out by the best man we can find for the job. We think you are that man.' He paused. 'What do you say? Will you return to Djakarta with me?'

I sighed heavily. 'Let me think about it, General,' I said. 'I'll be in touch with you some time in the next couple of days.'

Surabaya nodded gravely. 'I will await your reply.'

I was discharged the following morning, still sore all over and wearing my ribs taped up. There was a small bandage over my left cheek where the slight fracture there was healing, along with a deep laceration over it. I spent the best part of the day in my hotel room, mulling over Surabaya's offer. In a few more days I would be feeling fine again, I knew, so my physical condition should not deter me from taking the job.

The thing that still bothered me was the kind of job it was. Killing a man in the heat of battle was different from stalking him like an animal and shooting him down from ambush. I had never been involved in that kind of thing before, except as part of a military or para-military operation.

Besides, I wanted some time to recuperate from the beating I had taken from the cabby and his friend, and there would be no time for that if I accepted Surabaya's offer. Every day counted to him and the others on the People's Liberation Army death list. Nobody knew who was going to be next, either. It could be Surabaya himself, or even President Machmud.

I was still trying to decide, on my first evening out of the hospital. Ordinarily I would have passed it up at that time, and asked them to make their offer elsewhere. But fifty grand is a lot of money, and it was hard to turn it down. I could coast on that kind of capital for awhile, and take assignments that seemed less death-defying than some recent ones I had undertaken.

That consideration, plus a new development, made me give Surabaya an affirmative answer to his offer. I had just come out of a small restaurant early that evening, when I passed a news kiosk and saw the headline of the Hong Kong paper. FOURTH POLITICAL KILLING IN INDONESIA.

Since Surabaya had left Djakarta, the PLA had struck again. A Deputy Minister of Defense had been mysteriously murdered in his bed.

There was panic in high circles in Djakarta.

I returned to the restaurant to place a call to Surabaya. The government of Indonesia was in immediate danger of collapse if somebody did not do something. I seemed the most likely candidate. I called Surabaya and got him on the phone, and his voice was heavy with depression. The murdered man had been a friend of his.

'Was he on the death list?' I asked.

'Yes,' Surabaya said. 'And a couple of lesser persons on the list were bypassed for him. The only system in the killings seems to be availability of the victim at the time. Machmud could be next – or me.'

'You have a tense situation there, General,' I agreed. 'It seems that somebody is going to have to do something about it. Can you get us out of Bangkok early tomorrow?'

Surabaya's voice now sounded less heavy. 'You'll go?' he said to me.

'It sounds as if I may be sticking my head into a lion's mouth,' I replied. 'But I'll go.'

Surabaya was suddenly very emotional. 'We are grateful, Rainey,' he said.

I grunted in my throat. I had heard words like that before. They meant very little to me. 'Just have my fee ready in Djakarta,' I told him.

When I hung up, it was dark outside. I went out on the sidewalk to walk back to my hotel, my head buzzing with the implications of my commitment to Surabaya. I glanced down the street and saw the familiar-looking car.

It was the dented yellow taxi I had climbed into several nights ago across town. I was sure of it.

I moved closer, and saw the two heads. It was them all right, the same twosome. And I could see now that the car was a junked cab that had been fixed up some, to be made driveable. The cab number had been painted over. It was no wonder that the cab company had not been able to identify the fellow I described. He was not really a taxi driver.

Something tightened inside my gut, and I went on over to the taxi, coming up on the car from behind. I was not inebriated this time, and I was wearing my Star automatic under my lightweight suit jacket.

I opened the door of the taxi and climbed in behind them, before they saw me. They both turned quickly. Fat-belly the driver squinted hard at me, but did not appear to recognize me.

'Yes?' he said. 'You want to go somewhere, mister?'

I raised the Star up where they could see it, and they looked into its muzzle. 'Remember me?' I said darkly.

Recognition came to both of them at about the same moment. Long-face swallowed hard, and Fat-belly's mouth jerked at the corner.

'Hey,' Fat-belly said nervously. 'You look very healthy, mister. You don't hold no grudges, heh? We make it up to you.'

'Start driving,' I said. I pushed the muzzle of the Star up against his cheek, making the flesh bunch up there.

'We will return your money,' Long-face said cautiously, eyeing the Star.

'Start driving,' I repeated to Fat-belly.

He turned to the wheel. 'Okay, mister, okay. Where you want to go? I give you a nice tour, heh? No hard feelings.' He started the engine up.

'Just head out the way you took me the other night,' I said in a low growl.

Long-face glanced at me quickly. I aimed the gun at his nose. 'Face front,' I commanded.

They were both nervous as cats. The driver put the car in gear and pulled away, and I directed him onto a main boulevard. It was not long before we passed the Temple of the Reclining Buddha again, with its 160-foot deity outside the building. Then we were once more on the small street that led out of town.

It was the same kind of night as the other one, dark and quiet. I could not see their faces very well in the cab, but I knew they were both wondering how best to argue with a gun. I could have told them there was no way. I ordered the driver to accelerate his speed. He responded nervously. 100 KPH, and then 110. We were going well over a mile a minute, hurtling along the back street in the darkness, when I shoved the Star up behind Long-face's left ear. He winced.

'I am going to count to five,' I told them. 'If you have absented yourself from this vehicle by then, I won't kill you. Otherwise, I'll blow your face off.'

He turned partially toward me, sweat on his brow. 'But our speed! I cannot!'

'One,' I said.

Fat-belly let the car slow some.

'Keep it on 120 or you get it,' I growled at him.

The speed shot up again.

'Two,' I continued.

'Please!' Long-face breathed, watching the street hurtle past the car.

'Three,' I said deliberately, keeping the Star tight against the back of his skull.

'I will be killed!' he hissed out.

'Four.'

Suddenly, in desperation, Long-face yanked the door open beside him and hurled himself through it.

We were still on pavement, which was bad for him. I pulled the door closed and then glanced out the rear window. Long-face was tumbling head over heels wildly back there, limbs flailing awkwardly, as the pavement assailed him violently, breaking his bones and scraping the flesh off his body.

In a moment he was out of sight. I did not think the trauma would kill him, but I figured he would be in the hospital a hell of a lot longer than I had. And when he got out, he would probably be a cripple for the rest of his life.

'Okay,' I said to Fat-belly. 'You can slow it down now.'

We were getting close to the place where the two of them had taken me on that other night. I watched for the low building sitting by itself in the blackness, and finally we came to it. I directed Fat-belly to pull over.

'Please,' he said, as he stopped the car beside the dark building.

I got out as he turned the engine off. But as I walked around to his side of the car, around the rear of the vehicle, suddenly the engine roared again. I swore under my breath. I thought he would pull ahead and try to drive away, but then the car was hurtling back toward me.

Fat-belly was trying to run me down. He must have figured it was the only sure way of getting away from me and my Star.

I yelled an obscenity and threw myself to the road surface and the left rear wheel brushed my arm in roaring past. The tires kicked up dust from the roar and I glimpsed Fat-belly's face, twisted with desperation as he went past.

I rolled away, and came up with the Star aimed at Fat-belly's head. I fired too quickly and the hot lead bounced loudly off metal beside his head. He had the car in gear now, and the headlights were heading for my face and body.

The big tires came, and I rolled quickly again, hurting the healing ribs, and this time the bumper grazed my flailing arm, but the wheels again narrowly missed crushing me as the car thundered past.

This time Fat-belly kept going. The car squealed rubber and headed down the road and out of town. I rolled onto my belly and held the Star with both hands and aimed carefully this time, at the rear tire on the left. The car swerved around a rut, and the slug hit the front left instead, and I could hear the tire blow as the taxi kept swerving, went out of control, and drove into a utility pole about a hundred yards down the road.

There was an ear-splitting crash as he hit, and a sound of rending metal and breaking glass. The pole snapped off at waist level and came down on top of the car, smashing it like a bug.

I walked down to the wreck. The torn wire from the pole was snapping and crackling and making blue sparks, but the car had not caught on fire. I looked in through the window, and saw Fat-belly. The pole had missed crushing him through the car's roof, but he had impacted with the windshield in the crash, and was beyond help. His face was mangled beyond recognition, and his scalp lay back over the back of his head, exposing bone.

Fat-belly had mugged his last victim.

I limped off in the direction of a parallel street, a quarter-mile away. I did not want to be there when the police found the wreck.

I had business in Djakarta.

Two

Djakarta was hotter than Bangkok, but it seemed less congested with people and traffic. Surabaya and I arrived in the late afternoon, and there had been an army parade at Merdeka Square just a few hours earlier, apparently a desperate show of strength by President Machmud. It was some kind of holiday, and there were ceremonial dances going on at the Indonesian Opera House and the Hotel Indonesia. I knew that the best restaurants – the Bamboo Den and the Nirwana – and most of the smaller places along the Djuanda and Madjahapit were undoubtedly serving up their very best *sate* and *rijsttafel* and *babi guling* for the festive occasion.

Even with all that going on, though, there was a mood of tension in Djakarta. An undercurrent of fear was in the air, distinct and heavy.

Even the lowliest peasant was beginning to understand that a reign of terror had begun.

I did not check in at any of the big hotels. I did not even ride into the city with Surabaya, nor get off the plane with him. The last thing I wanted was to be spotted as an enemy of PLA even before I had gotten my bearings in Djakarta.

I got a small room on my own, at a guest house near downtown, by early evening, and by mid-evening Surabaya had arranged a meeting of myself, Surabaya, President Machmud, and Minister of Foreign Affairs Asaban. The meeting took place that very evening, within an hour of the arrangement by Surabaya.

It was clear that they felt there was no time to lose.

I insisted on having the meeting at my temporary room, rather than at Machmud's office in the National Palace or some other government building that might have someone watching it. Surabaya was a little perturbed by this, but Machmud came quite willingly. They all arrived together just before ten p.m., and all wore dark sunglasses and plain clothes. Nobody saw them arrive, I was certain.

By 10.10, we were seated in my small room at the guest house, Machmud on a short sofa and Surabaya near him on a straight chair. Dr Asaban preferred standing, and so did I.

'Well, Rainey,' Machmud said to me after we were situated. 'I can't tell you how relieved we are that you could come.' He was as tall as Surabaya, but much slimmer, and gave the appearance of a scholar or professor, with his wire-rim spectacles.

It seemed odd to be jammed together in that small room, with its spartan furnishings, with the President and Minister of Foreign Affairs of Indonesia, and one of its top-ranking military men.

'I'm glad I could make it, Mr President,' I told him.

Asaban spoke up then. 'The general has spoken highly of you, Mr Rainey,' he said in an oily, slick-smooth voice. He was shorter than either Machmud or Surabaya, and on the dumpy side, and looked very oriental, with pronounced epicanthic folds across his eyes. I did not like him much.

'The general is a gracious man,' I responded. 'I hope I can help you out here. But first I'm going to have to know a lot more than I do now.'

'Of course,' Machmud said. 'As the general may have mentioned, this deadly plot against us started in Palembang, over on Sumatra. Indonesia is a far-flung and diverse nation, Rainey, strung out between the South China Sea and the Pacific. In Djakarta we have modern buildings and air conditioning and traffic policemen. But there are still elephants and even rhino in our jungles, and a survivor of stone-age man on Sulawesi. The men you will be after are as diverse in personality as this island nation, Rainey, and each is dangerous in a different way.'

'I don't even know who they are yet,' I reminded him. 'Except for the labor organizer Amir Malik, whose apartment yielded the details of the PLA plot to you.'

'There are four other killers,' Dr Asaban said harshly, 'and they all must die!'

Machmud continued in his more temperate tone. 'Yes, there are five in all, Rainey. In addition to Malik, there are Nur Afandi, colonel in our First Army; Ibn Solkar, our Deputy Police Commissioner here in Djakarta; Ahmad Rahimat, an influential lawyer who has defended Communists on previous occasions; and perhaps the most insidious of them all, Ali Quan, the ex-Assembly leader and avowed leftist.'

'I myself recommended Colonel Afandi's promotion less than a year ago,' Surabaya said bitterly.

'And I have played golf with Rahimat at the local country club,' Asaban grumbled.

'I know, gentlemen,' Machmud said. 'I have had Quan in my home as my guest. At one time I thought of offering him a post in my cabinet, to show the leftists how moderate a man I am.' He laughed drily. 'As for Ibn Solkar, the policeman, he has always evidenced an open dislike for me, and accused me of trying to get him fired from his post. But I did not think he was dangerous. I did not think of any of these men as killers.'

'Why do you say Ali Quan is possibly the most dangerous?' I asked Machmud.

'Quan is known to have been involved in the 1968 coup attempt by the Communists,' said Machmud. 'But there was never any hard evidence against him. And it was he who organized the infamous meeting at Palembang a short time ago, and recommended this orgy of assassinations in preparation for the PLA's assumption of power.'

I began pacing the room slowly, and the three big-wigs were silent now, watching me. Surabaya had already advised me that all five of the plotters could be located in Djakarta or its environs, so there would probably be little traveling to do. It would be a close-in, deadly contest between two groups of assassins, and the ones who were most proficient at their work would win it and take all the Indonesian marbles.

And it would all happen, I guessed, within the next week or so. It was not the kind of struggle that dragged out. Fast action and the element of surprise were the keys to success on both sides.

'You mentioned working with other men,' I said suddenly to Surabaya.

Surabaya nodded. 'We felt that it is too big a job for one man. You would be going against a sophisticated organization that has its plans well coordinated.'

'I'll agree with that,' I said. 'If you wanted one man dead, I would probably go it alone without question. Five is different. The trouble is, the more people involved, the less control you have, and the more danger of betrayal, inadvertent or otherwise.'

Machmud nodded. 'That is why we thought we would start you out with just two men, Rainey, who would be completely under your command. We have a couple of men in mind, as a matter of fact, who should fill the bill nicely.'

'And who are they?' I asked.

Dr Asaban, the professor turned politician, spoke up again. 'One of them is a professional mercenary like yourself, Mr Rainey,' he said in the oily voice. 'Except that he is an experienced political assassin who has a rather formidable reputation in Europe and South America. His name is Michel Chaban, and he is a French national who travels on a Swiss passport. I picked him myself,' he added a little smugly.

I rubbed my chin. 'A professional assassin,' I mused.

'The other man,' Surabaya continued, 'is a man right out of the ranks of the Presidential Guard, a young officer who has served under me with distinction and who, as a young lieutenant, helped put down the uprising of 1968. He is pure Indonesian, and he has been an instructor in the martial arts and in the use of small weapons. He knows a lot of ways to kill a man, Rainey, and he should be of considerable help to you. His rank is captain.'

'You, of course,' Machmud told me, 'will be given the rank of full colonel in the Presidential Guard, a temporary commission that will last through this mission. Chaban will be regarded as captain. There will be no other men above or below you three in this special unit, unless you request them. And you will have complete control. Not even I will interfere, Rainey. You will report either to General Surabaya or myself directly.'

I thought all that through. 'All right,' I finally said. 'Two men sounds about right. But I reserve the right to fire either or both of them at any time, Mr President, or go it alone if I think that's right.'

Asaban raised his dark eyebrows, but Surabaya smiled, and Machmud nodded his approval. 'Very well, Rainey,' Machmud said. 'You are in charge of the operation.'

'Good,' I said. 'What about the guns the PLA hired at Palembang? The professional killers?'

'We have the description of one of them. He was seen leaving the Deputy Minister of Defense's residence after the killing there. But we do not know the names. We think there must be three or four. Do not concern yourself about them unless they get in your way, Rainey,' said Machmud. 'If you accomplish the job we've set for you, these hirelings will run in all directions. We will take care of any who are left. You get the leaders of the plot, and your job is finished.'

I nodded. 'It's a deal, Mr President,' I said.

In the next twenty-four hours I got a cram course on the PLA five, at the headquarters of the Presidential Guard, a Dutch colonial building not far from the National Palace. I was given a biographical brochure on each man, and was asked to familiarize myself with it so that I knew the PLA leaders' backgrounds almost as well as my own. I was taken to a slide projection room, and was shown a series of photographs of each man, until I was certain I could identify any of them if I saw them on the street. I was filled in then on the personal habits of each of the leaders, and the daily routines they followed. By the afternoon of that first full day, I had a pretty good idea of whom I was going after. I still, however, had not met the men who would be working under me. Surabaya was to take me to meet with them that evening. As we came down the corridor from the last orientation room, in preparation to leaving the building, we were still discussing Ali Quan, the suspected organizer of the assassination plot, when we received quite a surprise.

Quan and Rahimat – the powerful lawyer who was listed as one of the PLA plotters – almost walked into us at a corridor intersection on the main floor of the building.

I recognized both men immediately, because of my all-day familiarization course. Quan and Rahimat were as surprised as we were, but no embarrassment was shown on either side. I was amazed by the congeniality of it all.

'Well, General!' Quan said loudly, in a booming voice. He

was a squat, barrel-shaped man with coal black hair and the look of a Sumi wrestler. 'What a pleasant surprise!'

Surabaya clapped Quan on the shoulder. 'Quan, you old devil, what are you doing here in my secret lair?'

They were speaking in Bahasa Indonesian, and a lot of it was getting past me. But their outward friendliness did not escape me.

'Oh, it's just routine business,' Quan replied. 'Some leftist demonstrators have complained of brutality by guards at the Palace. Some of them are the children of my good friends. You know how it is. I am here to file a small complaint, with the help of my attorney, Mr Rahimat. I believe you've met.'

'Oh, yes,' Surabaya beamed widely. 'Mr Rahimat is one of our most skillful defense lawyers, I'm told.' He extended his hand to Rahimat, and Rahimat took it.

'Good to see you again, General.' He was a middle-aged man of medium height, but thin, and he had hard, intelligent eyes. His hair was graying.

Surabaya shook Rahimat's hand as if they were long-lost friends. Then he switched to English. 'Allow me to introduce Mr Richards from Canada,' he said, touching my arm. 'Here to study our humble security system, on an exchange program. I believe you helped develop it while in the Assembly, Quan.'

Quan's eyes narrowed just slightly, then he extended his hand to me, and I took it. 'Yes, a good program,' he said. 'Glad to meet you, Mr Richards.'

His handclasp was crushing. He had a lot of strength under all that heft. Rahimat shook my hand, too. It was all a little weird to me. I had been carefully instructed in the details necessary to the killing of these men on that very afternoon.

Rahimat struck the only minor chord, as he shook my hand.

'Are you certain, General, that Mr Richards is not another of your infamous CIA friends?'

Surabaya laughed loudly, as if it were a big joke. Quan and Rahimat joined in.

'I'm afraid not, Mr Rahimat,' Surabaya replied. 'Mr Richards is a policeman from Toronto.'

'And a very ordinary one at that,' I added.

Quan was still grinning, but he was studying my face through the grin. 'Well, General,' he said, 'give my best to Nabi Machmud when you see him.'

'Of course,' Surabaya said. 'And ask my people to bring your complaint to my personal attention, will you?'

'Thank you, General,' said Quan.

A moment later, they were heading on down the corridor, and we turned the corner and they were out of sight.

'Damn,' I said.

'Yes, it was an unfortunate coincidence,' Surabaya agreed. 'Also, one has to wonder what their real purpose is, in visiting my headquarters.'

I glanced over at Surabaya, and his face was grave. 'You're on their list, General,' I reminded him.

He stopped in the wide reception area and turned to me, and sighed heavily. 'That thought had crossed my mind,' he agreed.

That evening at eight I took a cab to the Officers' Club, which was near the American Embassy on Medan Merdeka Selatan. We got on the Djalan Pos for a while, the big boulevard that runs through the center of Djakarta, and there was quite a lot of pedestrian and bicycle traffic on the night streets. All the cafes were open, and most were filled with customers. There was still a carnival atmosphere in the city, one that seemed bizarre in light of the grim life-or-death maneuverings that were occurring on the political level.

I met Surabaya and Dr Asaban at the Officers' Club, in a back room and in secret, and we discussed the encounter of the afternoon. Surabaya was to take me across town to meet with the two men who would be working with me, when our meeting was over.

Asaban considered Quan and Rahimat's visit to the Presidential Guard headquarters as evidence of their acceleration of their coup plans, and wanted me to do something about them immediately. He was exhibiting the panic I had expected to meet in Djakarta, though Surabaya and Machmud were remarkably calm about their situation.

I promised Asaban that I would discuss possible actions against the PLA leaders that very evening, upon my first meeting with the two gunmen who were to work with me. He seemed somewhat soothed, but still very nervous.

It was when we all left together, through a little-used rear door leading to a dark parking area, that it happened. Asaban had insisted on walking to his car in our company, since he had no bodyguard with him. I thought it was a bad idea, but it was his life on the line.

When we got out onto the parking lot, just the three of us alone, the attack came suddenly and swiftly. A car pulled up near us from nowhere, with no lights on, and four men jumped out of it, armed with revolvers. They were tough-looking orientals, and they looked like they meant business.

'*Get down!*' I yelled at Surabaya and Asaban.

The firing began amid a flurry of obscene yelling by the gunmen. I threw myself against Surabaya, who was closest to me, and we went down together near a parked car. Asaban was still on his feet through it all, and did not seem to know how best to protect himself. The foursome all began firing at once, their revolvers blazing in the darkness, the banging resounding in my ears as I rolled away from the line of fire and found cover behind the parked Fiat near us, reaching for my Star at the same time.

In the first few seconds, my right arm was grazed, Surabaya was hit in the left thigh, and Asaban took two slugs in the chest and belly. Asaban went down heavily right out in the open, then a couple of the gunmen concentrated their fire on him.

I yelled at Surabaya again, then fired off two rounds at the nearest gunman, who was aiming toward Surabaya. The Star barked out loudly and the gunman was hit in the high chest and the face, just under the right eye. He did a backwards somersault and hit against the wheels of the car he had just climbed out of.

Asaban was hit several more times in those next few seconds, in the chest and belly, and I knew it was too late to save him. A couple more shots chipped pavement just beside Surabaya, then I found a second target and hit another gunman, this time in the groin. He returned fire while the remaining two clambered back into the waiting car. I fired the Star again and hit him in the chest, and he toppled onto his side. The gunmen in the car now fired off a few random shots as the black Mercedes roared off, and one caromed off metal beside my head.

I jumped to my feet and hurdled Surabaya's supine figure,

then fired three times after the departing car. The slugs banged off metal and one shattered the rear window, but I missed hitting the men inside. Then the car was squealing rubber on a dark side street, and disappearing in the night.

I had looked for a license plate, but there had not been one on the car.

I turned to Surabaya, who was struggling to his feet, his square face pale. 'Good God!' he said to me in English.

'Is it just the leg?' I asked.

'Yes.' He leaned against the damaged parked car.

I went over to the lifeless Asaban, feeling my arm. It was just a scratch I had taken. That was good, because I did not need any more injuries to have to heal from. I bent over Asaban, and felt for a pulse. There was none. His eyes were wide and staring, and there was blood all over his suit and on the pavement under him. They had gotten him good.

They had found their fifth victim.

They had apparently hoped to get both Surabaya and Asaban in this try. I doubt that their plans included me. Yet.

A couple of wide-eyed army officers came out of the rear door of the Officers' Club, and several pedestrians were gathering on the street. I turned to the army men.

'Get an ambulance!' I yelled at them in Indonesian.

One of them turned and went back inside. I went over to Surabaya. 'Asaban is dead,' I said.

'Oh, no,' he moaned.

'I have to get out of here. Call Chaban and Batak and tell them we'll make it another time. Maybe tomorrow. I'll be in touch.'

'But Rainey – '

'See you, General,' I said.

Then I hurried off into the darkness.

Three

The next morning the newspapers were full of the accounts of the assassination of Dr Asaban, and the attempt on Surabaya's life. I moved into a dormitory-type room in a closed down military annex building, a small place just off Djalan Nusantara, in accord with arrangements by Surabaya, and called Surabaya at the military hospital and told him to have my two underlings there with their personal effects by two p.m.

Surabaya said he had spoken to President Machmud on the phone not long before my call, and that Machmud was very upset. I could see why. PLA and its secret gunmen were much too successful in their undertakings. They should have had no way of knowing that Surabaya and Asaban and I were at the Officers' Club that evening, but they had. They obviously had an excellent grapevine for information, and it was helping them make their kills.

If I did not do something soon, it would be too late. Machmud was only too aware of this, and it came through in Surabaya's report to me about their conversation. As an afterthought, Machmud had congratulated me on my killings of two of the assassins – I had realized when I left Surabaya on the parking lot that they were beyond questioning – but I suspect his enthusiasm was strained.

At mid-morning I made a few select phone calls around town, asking questions about Amir Malik, the labor organizer who had led leftist demonstrations against the government openly in recent years, and in whose apartment was found the evidence that implicated him and the four others in the multiple-assassination plot.

Malik was an avowed Communist, as was Rahimat. He had been to Peking as a young man, where he had soaked up Maoist ideology. He denied any connection with Peking now, however, and protested that he had no notions of forceful change of government. Like the other PLA leaders, he lied a lot.

The thing I did not understand was why these five men suddenly decided to go on such a violent campaign to get what they wanted in Indonesia, when Machmud had been reasonably tolerant of their leftist protests. It was as if they had been prodded from outside, and the logical source was Peking. But Machmud had already denied any evidence of such involvement.

It was pretty clear, though, what PLA hoped to gain from the assassinations. The officials and military men on the list almost all had known leftists under them in a position to move up when the posts were vacated, with a little luck and a lot of pressure from the PLA. Machmud's vice president was conservative, like him, but a weakling who could be pushed around after Machmud was gone.

One of my mid-morning calls had nothing to do with business, but turned out to be the one most valuable to me, in the long run, in learning how the Palembang conspiracy got started just when it did. I had been in Djakarta about three years before, and had met a sweet little olive-skinned beauty named Nellie Ullah then, at an embassy cocktail party. She had been a ministry clerk at the time, and every man within range of her was trying to get her into bed. I had come close myself at that party, but someone had inadvertently intervened at a crucial moment, and I had had to say goodbye to Nellie without tasting of her obviously succulent fruit.

On that morning in Djakarta, I called her only to find out if she was still single and available, and to ask her if I might see her before I left town – after my assignment was finished. Assuming it would get finished.

Nellie was delighted to hear from me, and remembered me immediately. She was leaving town later that day, and asked if I might stop by her place before she left. I replied in the negative, but then remembered that there was little left to do until 2.00, when I met the men I was to work with. I told her I would be there in twenty minutes. I figured it was a raincheck acceptance for that aborted love-play at the embassy party, and just what I needed after the thing of the evening before.

I arrived at Nellie's place just after 11.00. She had a comfortable little apartment on the south side of the city, complete with ceiling fans and louver shutters at the windows and bamboo walls. Nellie herself was attired in a Chinese-style *cheong-sam* that fit her curved body nicely and was slit high up on her thighs.

'Well,' she said with a coy smile at the door. 'Jim Rainey.'

'Hi, Nellie,' I said.

I stepped inside and she closed the door behind me, and I just stood and looked at her for a long moment. She looked even better than she had before – the curves were fuller, and there was a general sexiness about her that was overpowering.

'You are looking good, Jim,' she told me.

I knew that it was not cautious of me to come to a girl who knew my real identity, in the middle of this other thing. But I figured Nellie was the kind of girl I could count on to keep quiet about something if I asked her to. At least temporarily.

'You're looking incredible,' I replied.

She flashed the big smile I had been dazzled by before. 'I don't have much time to stay,' I said.

'We don't need a lot of time,' she said. 'Do we?'

That was what I liked about oriental girls. They laid it on the line. The smile might be coy, but the style was not.

'No more than we would have on that party night,' I said, grinning. I could not take my eyes off her. The *cheong-sam* clung to her like it was painted on, and she appeared to be wearing nothing under it.

She got us some brandy and we sat together on a long, plush sofa in the middle of the room. The ceiling fan moved above us. We spoke of jasmine-odorous nights and moonlight through shutters and multi-hued moths around yellow lamps, and then the brandy was gone. Nellie reached across me to deposit her glass on an end table, and caressed me with a full breast. I loved it. I grabbed her and pulled her warm lips to mine and tasted of them.

'Mmm,' I said.

'I wondered if it would be the same,' she said.

'And?'

'It is, Jim. Just the same.'

'It's too bad we were interrupted before.'

She nodded. 'Perhaps we may be luckier this time?' she said.

I had never had a more open invitation. I reached around her and unzipped the *cheong-sam* dress and it fell off her shoulders. I pulled it down over the mounds of her breasts until she was nude to the waist. She was ripe. I leaned her back on the sofa and kissed her lips, and then moved down to the breasts. She gasped slightly in pleasure. My hand had found the slit in the *cheong-sam* and was now caressing her velvety inner thigh. The hand moved on up and there was nothing between it and Nellie up there.

'Ohh, Jim,' she breathed heavily.

I had been going to make a production of it – undress her casually, and then disrobe myself. But suddenly I was on fire. There could be no more waiting, even for those small formalities. Three years had been too long. I had thought of her often in the interim, probably more often than I remembered.

Nellie was suddenly on her back on the long sofa, and I knew I had forced her there. The *cheong-sam* was up around her hips and was revealing some of Nellie's nicest places. I fumbled with my trousers just for a moment, and then there was a sweet union.

'Oh, God, Jim,' she whispered harshly.

But I was beyond paying attention to small talk. I had not known, myself, how big a hunger I had built for Nellie in those three years. Not even when I made the phone call.

'*Djalan pelahan-pelahan,*' she breathed, lasping into her native tongue.

It was too late, though, to go slowly, even if I had wanted to. There was only the union now – the hot, tingling grasp of it, and the labored breathing of the girl whose breasts swelled under me, and then the explosion of primordial lust.

I did not leave her immediately when we were finished.

'*Djangan bergerak,*' she breathed into my ear, asking me to maintain the union.

I did, and we lay there together for a long time, enjoying the anti-climax that was still so intimate. Then I was lying beside her on the sofa, with her body cuddled into my arm.

'We were both three years ready,' I said to her.

'You have been one of my favorite fantasies, in my lonely

hours, since you left me that night,' she admitted.

'That's a nice thought,' I grinned.

We lay there. It was still only just past noon, and I had a little time before I had to leave, so I just enjoyed her nearness – the feel and smell of her.

'Why are you in Djakarta, lover?' she finally asked me. I had been anticipating that she would. 'There is no war here. Or is there?'

I grinned slightly. 'Not in the usual sense,' I said.

She propped herself up. 'Hey! You are here to help stop the assassinations, aren't you?' She knew I was a professional soldier, and she was a smart girl.

'Please don't express that opinion to anybody else, Nellie,' I told her.

'I wouldn't, Jim, you know that.'

'Or mention my name to anybody. I'm using an alias.'

'You *are* here to help!' she said, smiling happily.

'I can't tell you why I'm here,' I said. 'And I don't want you to mention me to any of your friends. Okay?'

'Okay,' she said. She resumed slowly. 'But if you were in Djakarta to help find these assassins who terrorize our government, I might be able to give you some information that would help you.'

I turned to the half-nude girl, my face serious now. 'And just how would that be?' I said.

'At a party a couple of nights ago, at the Chinese Embassy, I heard a short conversation I was not supposed to hear. An informant was telling a Foreign Affairs Ministry employee that he knew something important about the assassinations, and would sell it for the right price.'

'What was the response?' I asked.

'The employee to whom he made the offer seemed too frightened to pursue the matter. I went to an embassy host and got the name of the informant, and it turned out he is an airline ticket clerk who used to be a civil servant. His name is Abu Phanko, and I have looked up his address.'

I made a careful mental record of the name. I figured if Nellie could get the address, I could too, and I did not ask her what it was.

'Why haven't you gone to the police or the army about this?' I said to her.

She shrugged. 'I, too, am afraid, Jim. If I go to the wrong people, I could end up in the bay with my throat cut. Who knows who are rebels and who are not?'

'I'm a professional,' I said. 'Did it ever occur to you that I might have been hired to fight for the Communists?'

She looked at me as if I had made a rather insane suggestion, and then laughed lightly. 'Oh, Jim! You may fight for pay, but you have scruples. You would not engage in cold-blooded murder for profit.'

Even though my assignment was defensive in nature, I wondered just how far from that description of the PLA activities I really was. I rose and adjusted my clothing and prepared to go. Nellie sat up on the sofa and pulled the *cheong-sam* down around her thighs but did not cover her bosom. Her people had been going around bare-breasted for centuries, anyway, and still did out in the boondocks, so she had little modesty in that regard.

'You did not comment,' she said.

I sighed. I did not want her to know enough to hurt either her or me. 'I'm not in the pay of the Communists, Nellie. I'm here on business that I can't discuss with you. That's all I can tell you.'

'Can you tell me whether my information might help you?' she asked innocently.

'Anything is possible,' I said.

She smiled knowingly. 'Okay, Jim. I understand.'

'I hope you do,' I said.

At 2.00 p.m. I was back at the abandoned-annex room. Chaban showed at 2.10 with no apology for his tardiness. I did not like that beginning. Batak did not show at all.

Chaban came into the room filled with arrogance and aloofness, a dark-complexioned Frenchman who was as tall as me, but slightly slimmer. He wore a tailored suit and looked like a male fashion model. It was obvious he had made some money in his chosen profession. He had dark hair and was fairly handsome, but his eyes had a brittle hardness in them that could be unnerving.

'Well,' he said in accented English. 'The infamous Jim Rainey.

Did you really kill Joe Maltese?'

I closed the door behind him and turned to him. We met eye to eye.

'Does it really matter?' I said flatly.

He raised his dark eyebrows. 'No offense, Rainey. Maybe a drink would relax you. Do we have anything here?'

I turned from him without replying and went to the middle of the room. There was a slow-moving ceiling fan overhead that barely moved the hot air. At the end of the room were three cots, and there was a stove and sink on one wall. A table stood under the fan, with four bamboo-and-reed chairs sitting at it. There were two windows on one wall, and they were shuttered against the sun. Stripes of sunlight slashed through them, though, and fell diagonally along the floor at my feet. Somewhere in the room a mosquito buzzed, and the thought occurred to me that we had no netting.

'Chaban,' I said slowly, still faced away from him. 'I thought you and Batak were to arrive together?'

'Ah, Batak,' he said. He came and stood beside the table. He wiped a finger through a light layer of dust on its surface, and made a small face. 'We had an altercation at Guard headquarters, just after leaving the general.'

'An argument?' I said.

'A small one. It seems that Batak despises men like me, who deliver death for a payment.'

I studied Chaban. 'Where is he now?' I said.

'He indicated he was headed for the Spice Islands Bar,' Chaban said acidly. 'A dirty place for natives only.'

That was the kind of remark I would have expected from Chaban, in the brief time I had spoken with him. I was with Batak. I had absolutely no affection for professional killers. And I would not have liked Chaban if he had been an accountant. 'Sit down, Chaban,' I said to him.

Chaban regarded me imperiously, then seated himself grudgingly at the table. I sat across from him. 'I've been reading up on you,' I told him seriously. 'You're regarded as a highly efficient killer, it seems.'

He shrugged and grinned a very hard grin. 'We all have our little skills, eh?'

I leaned back on my chair. 'You're also very quick on the trigger, Chaban. Sometimes you kill when it's unnecessary.'

The grin faded. 'Who is to say what is necessary?' he asked deliberately.

'In this mission, I will say,' I told him. 'If you can't accept that, you'll be out of this very quickly.'

Anger flickered in Chaban's eyes. He was apparently not accustomed to being spoken to in that way. 'Yes?' he said darkly.

I leaned forward toward him. 'Yes. There are those who would lump us pretty much together, Chaban, you and me. But I have to tell you that I don't. I'm a soldier. I've never worked with a hired killer before, and would not be now if Surabaya were not so high on you. If you play this thing my way, we'll get along. If you don't, we won't.'

Chaban grunted in his throat. 'I appreciate your frankness, Rainey.' His face fell into hard, straight lines. 'Now let me be, also. I have told Surabaya that I think it was wrong of him to put you in charge of this multiple killing. This is my kind of job, Rainey, not yours. I am the expert in what we undertake to accomplish in the next week or so – not you. I know how to get to one man quickly and quietly. I should be running this operation, Rainey. I will submit to Surabaya's authority, and acknowledge you as the *de facto* leader of this group. But I will not be told how to practice my chosen profession by a part-time soldier who plays at war and meddles in things he knows little about.'

I met his hard stare with my own. I felt like firing him right on the spot. But I knew how short time was. 'The first time you disobey a direct order, Chaban,' I said evenly, 'you'll be off the team. Is that clear?'

Chaban let the hard smile return to his lips. 'I think we understand each other, Rainey,' he said arrogantly.

I swallowed my anger back. If I intended to try to do what Machmud and Surabaya wanted, I was going to need both Chaban and Batak very quickly. I had already gathered information on Malik that would allow us to make a move against him, and I had to check out the alleged informant Phanko that Nellie had mentioned to me. There was plenty of work to be done, and immediately.

I glanced at my watch. 'Well, it appears as if Batak isn't coming. We'll discuss procedure later, after I've found him. I'll try the Spice Islands Bar first.'

'He will undoubtedly be there,' Chaban said. 'But you are surely not going after him, Rainey?' he said sarcastically.

'Why not?'

He shook his head. 'A white man does not go running after a wog in this part of the world. They will lose respect for you if you do.'

I glowered at Chaban. 'And forget their place, you mean?' I said.

'Exactly,' Chaban replied casually.

I was beginning to see why Batak had chosen not to come there with Chaban. I rose and went to the door. 'If I can convince Batak to work with a bastard like you,' I said, 'I'll be back.'

The Spice Islands Bar was a big barny place open to the street and with many exotic odors besides liquor present, not all of which were pleasant ones. There was a small afternoon crowd there, a group of Portuguese sailors off a freighter and a few locals. I found Batak, still in his khaki uniform, at the rear of the place, sitting on a barstool. He had several glasses near him on the bar, all empty, but he did not appear inebriated.

I took a stool next to him, and he glanced over at me.

'Feeling any better?' I asked him.

He squinted at me. He was a burly young fellow, under thirty, and he looked very Indonesian, with a broad face and an olive complexion. The part of his arms that showed below his short-sleeved khakis was all muscle. A scar began under his strong chin on the left side and ran down out of sight under his shirt collar. He looked every bit as tough as I had been told he was.

'Are you Rainey?' he asked suspiciously.

'The same,' I said. 'Chaban said I'd find you here.'

'Ah, Chaban!' He fairly spat the words out. He spoke better English than the Frenchman who had such a low opinion of him.

'I know what you mean,' I said.

He turned to regard me studiously. 'You're saying you don't like Chaban?'

'Not from what I've seen so far.'

He turned back to stare down at the empty glasses. 'I have run into his kind before,' he said, 'and I am not referring to the fact that he is a paid killer. He treats me – like a servant. Just because I am Indonesian and he is European.'

'I can imagine,' I said. 'He doesn't think much of me, either.'

Batak looked over at me again.

'He thinks I'm not qualified for the job ahead,' I went on. 'Hell, maybe he's right. But that doesn't make him any less of a sonofabitch.'

Batak's face changed slightly. 'He told you that?'

'In spades,' I said. 'Scout's honor. But the way I see it is, I'm going to have to put up with him for a while.'

He thought about that a moment, then grinned. 'You don't sound any more convinced than me, Rainey.'

'You've been thinking of quitting, haven't you?' I said to him confidentially.

He nodded. 'Frankly, yes.'

I sighed. 'I'm going to be frank with you, too, Batak. I need you. If only because we outnumber Chaban.'

He liked that. He grinned broadly now. 'You are not at all like I imagined you, Rainey. I thought you would be more like – well, Chaban.'

'Nobody is quite like Chaban,' I grinned. 'Can I buy you a drink to celebrate our temporary partnership?'

Batak hesitated only a moment. 'Sure, Rainey.'

I ordered two drinks from the bartender. There was some laughter from the sailors near us, which I ignored. Batak turned and listened to some of the banter in Portuguese, then turned back somber-faced. The drinks came and I lifted my glass to toast our new undertaking, but before I could do so, one of the sailors just behind me said something loudly in our direction. I turned briefly.

'What was all that about?' I asked Batak.

He sighed. 'I speak a little Portuguese. He said that you Americans were afraid to go into Angola to fight the Cubans there.'

I turned again, and the sailors laughed and jeered. I shrugged and turned back to Batak. 'To hell with them,' I said. 'Let's drink to our immediate and spectacular success against – '

A big sailor came up between Batak and me, and put his smelly face close to mine. 'Do you understand, Yankee?' he said in thickly-accented English. 'We say all Yankees are cowards!'

I threw the glass of liquor into his fleshy face.

He was taken completely by surprise. He coughed and wiped at his cheek for a moment, and suddenly the laughing had stopped behind us, and the big sailor was cursing me out in his native language. In the middle of it, he grabbed a bottle from the bar, smashed its neck off, and held it up to my face. I think he intended to gouge my eyes out with it. For a start.

Before I could do anything to defend, though, Batak casually reached over to the sailor and grasped his big shoulder in what seemed like a casual grip, and squeezed. The sailor's jaw flew open, his eyes bulged out, and he made a croaking sound in his throat. He grabbed at Batak's hand, and then fell against the bar and slipped to the floor.

I was impressed. Batak had not even moved off his barstool.

'How the hell did you do that?' I said.

Before he could reply, two sailors had attached themselves like bulldogs to Batak's back and shoulders, jamming him up against the bar. In the same moment, three more of them were all over me, hitting and kicking and gouging.

I found myself falling off the stool, and then hitting the floor. I was being punched and kicked repeatedly, but fortunately none of the blows had landed on my healing ribs. The local Indonesians apparently had just been waiting for a chance to have a go at the Portuguese sailors, because now they all got into the brawl, and it became a real free-for-all. Some of the sailors were pulled off Batak and me, and we were left with only a pair apiece. I pulled loose from one man and struggled to my feet while the other rained blows on my face and head. I found a bottle sitting on the bar, and swung it at him savagely and it smashed into his face, busting his nose and probably fracturing his jaw. I clearly heard bone breaking as he ran backwards and dived prettily over a table and chairs, taking them all down with him.

In the next split-second, while my other assailant was grabbing me from behind again, I saw one of the sailors on Batak, against the bar, draw a knife. Batak stopped a quick stabbing motion with his left hand, and then with a deft parry of his own, jammed stiffened fingers into the sailor's eyes. The right eyeball popped and a viscous fluid ran down onto the fellow's cheek. He turned, grabbing at his face, totally blind at that moment, yelling and screaming. He stumbled into the melee and was knocked down by somebody immediately.

The fellow behind me punched a hard blow into my back, and I grunted under the impact. I rammed an elbow back toward him, and connected with his throat, smashing his windpipe. He fell off me, against the bar, and clutched at his throat with both hands, his face going black, his mouth wide open to suck air in. He slid to the floor, gasping and making ugly sounds in his throat.

I wiped blood from my face and saw Batak tear loose from his other assailant and throw a backhand chop into the fellow's head that would have felled an ox. The sailor went stumbling in a circle away from Batak, then just stood there amid the flailing fists around him, out on his feet. Batak touched him lightly on the shoulder and the big sailor toppled onto his face like a tree. Batak glanced at me to see if I wanted more of this entertainment.

I shook my head, and gestured toward a rear door. We stepped past the still-wild melee, and edged our way to the rear door and through it. In a moment we had passed through a dirty back room and stood in a dusty alleyway behind the place.

We squinted in bright sunlight. Batak had a bruise on his cheek and a tear of his uniform shirt, but otherwise looked as if he had just come off parade. He looked at the drying blood on my face.

'They got to you, Rainey,' he grinned.

'I didn't see anybody hurting you,' I said. 'You were great in there.'

He shrugged. 'I was lucky. Those people were nasty.'

I grinned and slapped him on the shoulder. 'Come on back to our little home away from home. Maybe you can help me be lucky, too.'

Batak returned the grin. 'Why not?' he said.

Four

At that first meeting of the three of us, late that afternoon, Chaban was surprisingly jovial and solicitous. I thought it was a bit exaggerated, and knew it was a put-on for some obtuse reason. Batak would not return the joviality, and I did not blame him. He did not like working with Chaban, and made it clear he would be glad when it was all over with. I felt much the same way. I briefed them on what I had learned about the PLA five, and particularly Malik, and said I wanted to move against Malik in the next twenty-four hours, because he seemed easiest to get to, and his death might slow the others down some in their own plot. If we could put them on the defensive, I knew, we would have accomplished something important. When I spoke of these tactical matters, which I considered important, Chaban let me know how silly it all was by cleaning his Mauser 7.65 mm Parabellum automatic all through the discussion, hardly looking at me.

I left Chaban at the annex in late afternoon, and Batak drove me in our rented Fiat 1200 across town to the address of Abu Phanko, the civil service employee who claimed to know something about the assassination orgy that was terrorizing Djakarta. I knew that Phanko might have been joking with Nellie, or bullshitting her, or he might be a stooge of the PLA, trying to drag opponents of the coup into the open. But, as it turned out, Phanko was on the level.

I left Batak in the car on the street, and entered a rather run-down building where Phanko lived on the third floor. There was litter on the stairway, and roaches cavorting on the scarred walls. When I knocked on Phanko's battered door, I got an immediate response. A slim, emaciated fellow opened it and stared narrow-eyed at me.

'Yes?' he said.

'Mr Phanko?'

'I am.'

'I'm a friend of Nellie Ullah,' I said.

He narrowed the slitted eyes even more, then suddenly remembered her. 'Ah, yes. Nellie. A lovely girl.'

'She tells me you have information about the current rash of assassinations in Djakarta,' I said.

A flicker of fear came into his face. 'Who are you?'

'A friend of Nellie, like I said. And of the government.'

He hesitated, then moved aside. 'Please come in,' he said.

I entered a dirty, littered room with just a few pieces of beat-up furniture and an unmade bed in a corner. There were liquor bottles on a low table, but I did not smell any alcohol on Phanko's breath. He closed the door behind us, and turned to me.

'It is true, I have heard something that I am certain bears on the assassinations,' he said. He spoke in English with a very rhythmical, lilting accent. 'But I do not part with it for nothing, Mr – '

'Smith,' I told him. 'John Smith.'

'Ah,' he smiled. 'A common name in America, I understand.'

'How much do you want, Phanko?' I asked.

He hesitated, thinking. 'Ten thousand rupiahs,' he said very emphatically.

Even at the high exchange rate, that was much too much. 'I'll give you five thousand,' I said.

He shook his narrow face slowly. 'My price is firm, Mr Smith.' He smiled a wan smile. 'I know that Americans have much money to spend in these matters. I have been involved in information-selling before, you see. No, I will not take a rupiah less than ten thousand.'

I reached into my pocket and came up with a wad of bills. I counted out five thousand rupiahs and laid them on the low table nearby, then put the rest back into my pocket. 'I've just given you five thousand rupiahs for the information,' I said deliberately. 'A fair sum. In fact, a generous one.'

Phanko's jaw set. He had grit, for a little man. 'The price is still ten thousand rupiahs,' he said grimly.

I sighed. 'I don't think I'm getting through to you, Phanko. Let me see if I can put it another way.'

I kicked Phanko in the groin with my knee.

Phanko gasped loudly, doubling over and falling onto his side on the floor, grabbing at himself and grunting out noises. I let him do that for a minute, then went up beside him and grabbed him by his shirt and pulled him to his feet. I hurled him bodily across the room, and he crashed across the low table and upset it, and the rupiahs went flying. He hit the floor hard on his back, yelling again. I walked over and kicked him in the side. Phanko croaked out some more noises.

I stood over him menacingly.

'You sonofabitch,' I growled. 'You never made ten thousand rupiahs in a year. Now are you talking, or do I take the five grand back and keep at you anyway?'

Phanko could not talk very well at first, but when he could, he made it clear that he had had enough.

'All right,' he gasped. 'Five thousand.'

I went and sat on a straight chair. Phanko slowly climbed to his knees, and then decided to sit on the floor, with his five grand all around him.

'Let's have it,' I said. 'And listen, Phanko. It had better be straight. I mean it. I don't have the time to go off on any wild goose chases because of you. I'll kill you if you lie to me.'

He nodded understanding. 'You will get it just as I did.' He paused for breath. 'A man came to Djakarta just before the assassinations began. A Russian named Vasil Rublev. Supposedly a foreign service courier to the Russian embassy here. But almost as soon as he arrived, he flew to Palembang on the same plane with a known leftist, Ahmad Rahimat the lawyer.'

Ahmad Rahimat, I thought. One of the five PLA secret leaders who had planned these multiple assassinations. The fellow I had met fortuitously in the headquarters of the Presidential Guard, along with Ali Quan.

'Are you sure of this?' I said to Phanko.

'My source is unimpeachable,' he said. 'He is a friend who works for our foreign service and who has seen Rublev on a previous occasion, when Rublev came here on a brief mission. My friend thinks Rublev is a KGB agent.'

I nodded. 'Is that all?'

'Yes, except that Rublev is still in town.'

'At his embassy?'

'Oh, no. They report that he has left Djakarta. He is underground now.'

'Where?' I said.

'I have no idea. My friend saw him, though, just a couple of days ago, coming out of a restaurant.'

'What restaurant?'

Phanko squinted his eyes. 'I believe it was the Indonesia.'

I made a sound in my throat. 'Okay, Phanko.' I turned and walked to the door and opened it, then turned back to him.

'Enjoy the five grand,' I said sourly. 'You're not likely ever to get that much again at one time.'

He knew it. He looked away from me sheepishly. I left him sitting there on his littered floor.

Less than two hours later I was meeting with President Machmud himself, and General Surabaya, at Guard headquarters, in the private room we had used on previous occasions. This time I had left Batak at the dormitory room at the annex and taken Chaban with me, because I wanted to get a feeling for working with him. Batak was making some phone calls to see if he could get a lead on Rublev's whereabouts.

I left Chaban in the parking area behind the Guard headquarters, and he resented very much not being included in the meeting. I am certain he figured it was he who should be discussing this development with Machmud and Surabaya, rather than me. But I wanted him to keep an eye on the rear entrance of the building for us, to make sure the integrity of the meeting was secure.

When I got into the small white room with Machmud and Surabaya, Machmud was extremely upset.

'I don't understand this!' he was saying loudly, as he paced the floor like a tiger. 'I have leaned over backwards to keep on friendly terms with Russia! And now they send a man here to kill me!'

Surabaya turned heavily to me. He stood beside the conference table near me. He was still limping from his flesh wound in the thigh, but it was healing fast. 'We made some calls, Rainey,' he told me, 'one to your CIA in Washington. Vasil Rublev is not just KGB. He is from Mokri Dela, KGB's "bloody affairs" section.'

'Damn!' I said under my breath.

Machmud turned to me. 'This is a well-planned and coldly executed plot by Moscow to help PLA take over this government by force!' he said loudly. 'Force of the deadliest kind! You were right, Rainey, Quan and his cohorts *were* prodded into this ugly plot from outside. But not from Peking.'

I shook my head slowly. 'You've been on good terms with the Russians,' I said. 'Or so you thought.'

'I entertained their ambassador at my palace just a few weeks ago!' Machmud raged. 'After one of these murders had already taken place! These men were plotting my death while they ate my food at my table!'

I shrugged. 'The local ambassador might know nothing about it,' I said. 'Mokri Dela is pretty careful in the way they proceed. Their local embassy people may really think you're the best of friends. They might even think Rublev has returned to Moscow.'

'Either way, it is an outrage!' said Machmud, and then added an invective in Indonesian, as if English were not sufficient to vent his wrath.

'I agree, Mr President,' I told him. 'The question is, what do we do about it?'

Surabaya spoke up. 'I say we go ahead with our plan to rid ourselves of the PLA five,' he commented, 'just as quickly as possible. With them gone, the threat to Indonesia will also be gone. Then we may deal with Mr Rublev at our leisure. I suggest deporting him publicly, writing a protest to Moscow, and closing down their embassy here and cutting off all diplomatic relations with them.'

Machmud nodded. 'I would dearly enjoy holding this Soviet-backed plot up to world opinion.' He turned away angrily. 'No wonder Quan and his rabid colleagues had sufficient capital to hire professional gunmen, and the know-how to organize such a secret move against us. Moscow was supplying cash and know-how.'

'Then let us proceed as I suggest,' Surabaya said.

It was then that I intervened. 'General, if I may, I'd like to make a modification to your suggestion,' I said.

They both turned to look at me. 'I agree that we go ahead full-steam with our plan to liquidate your enemies. But I wonder how much effect would be made by deporting Rublev and accusing Moscow openly. They're masters at double-talk and confusion. They would deny loudly, and make counter-accusations, and that would be the end of it.'

'Are you suggesting we just ignore this bloody subversion?' said Machmud incredulously.

'Not at all, Mr President,' I replied. 'I suggest we add Rublev's name to our own death list.'

They both stared hard at me for a long moment. Finally, Machmud spoke. 'Kill a Russian KGB man?'

'That's what he's trying to do to you,' I said flatly.

A grin began crawling onto Surabaya's face. 'I like it,' he said in a conspiratorial voice. 'I like it very much.'

Machmud regarded Surabaya solemnly.

'There would be no front-page shouting this way,' I said. 'But you would have delivered a message to Moscow that they'll understand. Anybody who comes to Indonesia to shed Indonesian blood had better come prepared to defend himself to the death.'

'I like it,' Surabaya repeated.

'Also, you could let Moscow decide whether to close their embassy. If they leave it open, they'll have to swallow a little pride. If they close it, it's they who'll have to explain to the world why.'

Machmud was getting a small start of a grin on his face, too. 'By God, Rainey. You make much sense. Suddenly I think we are wasting your talents on an assassination mission.'

'Nothing is more important to Indonesia at this moment,' I told him, 'than to rid the country of your would-be killers, Mr President.'

Machmud nodded. 'You're right, of course, Rainey. And I accept your proposal to add Vasil Rublev to your death list. We'll add a sum to your fee, of course.'

'Of course,' Surabaya said.

I shook my head. 'I'm not Michel Chaban, Mr President,' I said. 'A job is a job. I don't count heads when it's all over. The fee you quoted already is very satisfactory.'

Surabaya raised his eyebrows, his square face etched with mild surprise. 'Just when I think I have you figured out, Rainey, you muddle my head about you,' he said.

I grinned. 'Good. I don't like to be too predictable,' I told him. 'That's the way to end up dead in my business.'

We all left the room together. There was no reason to suspect any danger on the parking lot, because Chaban was out there on guard. On the way out there, Machmud asked me how I was getting along with Batak and Chaban. I told him I liked Batak, but that I was having a hell of a time getting along with Chaban. He asked if I wanted to get somebody else, and I said there was no time. I told him I was going after Malik the very next day, and that if things went well, all five PLA killers would be dead at week's end.

Out on the parking area, Machmud spoke to Chaban, and Chaban responded with typical arrogance.

'I hope all is well with you, Chaban,' Machmud told him.

'It will be, Mr President,' Chaban said sourly, 'when the meetings are finished and the real work begins.'

Machmud did not respond to this criticism, but he and Surabaya exchanged looks. Machmud's limousine pulled up then, with a uniformed driver, and Machmud started to get in, when the driver climbed out and spoke to him.

'Mr President,' the short fellow who also operated as bodyguard said. 'I went into the building for a cup of coffee, and when I returned, the limousine's radiator was leaking. It has lost considerable water, but I am certain that we may drive back to the Palace without difficulty.'

'Well, old radiators spring leaks,' Machmud said. 'Have it repaired tomorrow, Yefru.'

'If you boil over, give my office a call,' Surabaya said, 'and I'll send a car.'

Machmud nodded and started to get into the Rolls limousine. But this time I stopped him.

'Just a moment, Mr President,' I said.

Machmud turned back to me.

'How long did you leave the limousine, Yefru?' I asked the chauffeur-bodyguard.

The short fellow shrugged. 'Just a couple of minutes. Well, perhaps five.'

That meant ten or fifteen. I turned to Machmud. 'Let me drive you back, Mr President. Chaban and I can drop you off. It's safer that way.'

Machmud glanced toward the slightly-hissing radiator. Yefru now had an indignant look on his face.

'This car is perfectly all right, Mr President,' he said.

Machmud thought a moment. In that moment, Chaban said, 'Rainey is right, Mr President.'

Machmud finally nodded. 'All right, I'll let you take me.'

'You can have Yefru leave the car here, to be checked out,' I suggested.

Yefru had gotten the idea, now, that we were concerned that the car had been tampered with. 'That is not necessary, Mr President,' he said stiffly. 'Nothing could have happened to the car in the brief time I was gone.' His Indonesian was almost too swift for me to follow. 'I will have a look at it upon my return.'

'Very well, Yefru,' Machmud said. He went over to the Fiat Chaban and I had come in, and said a few parting words to Surabaya, who was staying at the headquarters building a while yet.

Chaban followed Machmud to the Fiat, and they got in. Surabaya limped back to the building. I stood and watched Yefru start the big limousine, give me a hard look through the window, and drive away, the radiator still hissing slightly.

I had just started to follow Machmud and Chaban to the Fiat, when the explosion came.

The limousine had been only thirty feet away from me when it suddenly disintegrated in a violent eruption, a blast that assailed my ears savagely and knocked me to the pavement.

I hit hard, then turned to look at the limousine. It was engulfed in flames, what was left of it, with black smoke already curling into a night sky. The figure of the short driver now separated from that mass, aflame, and began running toward me and the Fiat. He was a human torch. A dull yelling issued from the depths of his throat as he ran past me, his arms waving frantically above his head. He fell between me and the Fiat, and then just lay there and burned. Machmud and Chaban were now out of the car, and Machmud was looking pale in the light from the flaming car.

I got up and went to the burning-out driver Yefru and threw my jacket over him, but it was too late. He was dead. Chaban turned quickly at the sound of a car engine starting, out on the street, and drew his gun.

'*Rainey!*' he yelled.

I nodded. '*Get back inside, Mr President!*' I yelled at him. Surabaya was staring, too, from the building, and I figured they would be safe together.

Chaban fired a shot toward the tire-squealing car out on the curb, and then climbed back into the Fiat. I piled in beside him and we roared out of the parking lot past the blazing limousine, bumping down a drive to the street. The other car, a black Mercedes, was half a block ahead.

We hurtled down the dark street after it, Chaban driving. He was good, and we steadily caught up with the fleeing car. I got a couple of shots off, but did not hit either of the two heads we could see inside. The car turned off the street and we followed, careening around a sharp corner. We did that a few more times, and were right on the tail of the Mercedes. A shot rang out from it and spidered our windscreen between our heads. I returned fire, and I must have nicked the driver, because the car swerved broadly, banged up over the curb, scraped loudly against a building wall, and then headed sharply back across the street. It went up over the far curb then, and swerved to a stop on the sidewalk.

Chaban skidded to a stop just thirty yards behind the Mercedes as both the men in it now piled out. One crouched and began firing toward us as we climbed out of the Fiat, and a slug narrowly missed my head and caromed off the metal roof of the Fiat. Chaban returned fire and hit the other man high in the chest, and he slammed against an open door of the Mercedes and slid to the pavement.

The first man now turned and began running toward an alleyway. 'I want him alive!' I yelled at Chaban.

Chaban gave me a look.

'I'll go around to the far end of the alley, and you cover this end,' I told him. Then I was running down a side street to intercept the other gunman at the far end of the alley.

I got there on the far street just as the gunman was emerging from the alley. I fired over his head with the Star, just to stop him. He returned fire wildly and ducked back into the alley, heading back toward Chaban. I raced down to the alley entrance and flattened myself against the building corner and looked down there. The gunman had run into Chaban near the other end.

The gunman fired at Chaban and just missed killing him. Chaban returned fire and knocked him down. I yelled to Chaban to hold it, as I came down to them.

But Chaban's anger had been aroused by the near miss. He now stood over the unarmed gunman, aiming the gun at his face. In the next instant, to my surprise, he fired and blew the side of the man's head off.

I stopped short of them, about ten yards away. 'Damn it, Chaban!' I yelled. 'Are you nuts, goddam it!'

Chaban turned casually to me, and he was in control again. I came on up to him, awaiting an answer.

'He was trying to kill me, Rainey. He would have nothing to tell us, anyway. He was a nothing. You will have to trust me in matters like this. I know best.'

I could not believe it. I holstered the Star carefully, gave Chaban a blistering look, and hauled off and knocked him down.

Chaban hit the pavement beside the man he had killed, a look of shock and surprise on his face. Blood seeped from the corner of his mouth. In a sudden frenzy, he drew the Mauser he had just holstered, and aimed it at my chest.

'Go ahead, you sonofabitch,' I said. 'But they'll never believe he killed me. They'll check the slug. You'll be out of a job here, and anywhere else in this part of the world.'

He slowly lowered the gun. Wiping at his mouth, he growled, 'Nobody does that to Michel Chaban.'

'I told you to spare him,' I said angrily. 'You chose not to. He might have helped us, damn it. I'm going to give you the benefit of the doubt this time. But don't let this kind of thing happen again, you bastard – or you're out.'

Chaban glared at me for a long moment, then holstered the Mauser and rose. Without further comment to me, he turned and headed back out of the alley, toward the Fiat.

4

I waited there a moment, standing over the corpse of the gunman who might have shortened the job ahead, trying to cool down inside. Then I followed Chaban to the car.

Five

Amir Malik was a rabid leftist labor organizer who was the vice-president of one of the largest labor unions in Indonesia. He had come up the hard way, starting out as a steward in a textile plant and then spending years making the rounds of non-union businesses, haranguing workers about the advantages of organization. There had been some head-cracking in those days, when he had gotten opposition from small employers, and Malik had spent a brief time in jail because of a disorder he led on a public street outside a manufacturing plant.

Now Malik was considered a man of importance in Indonesian labor relations, and it had been known for some time that he was a friend of Ali Quan when Quan was in the People's Consultative Assembly. He was also seen recently in the company of Ibn Solkar, the Deputy Police Commissioner of Djakarta and another of the PLA five implicated in the assassination plot.

Because Malik did not deem it necessary to keep a bodyguard with him, as Quan and Rahimat were doing more and more recently, and because his duties took him out into the open more, and he dined out in public with impunity, I decided it was Malik who would be our first hit.

I had had a man close to Malik for two days, a fellow who worked for the Indonesian Workers' Organization (IWO), but had some personal grudge against Malik himself. The morning after the bombing of President Machmud's car, I met with this fellow, whose name was Sarasin, at a coffee-house, and got the very latest on Malik.

I knew that the bomb blast had been an attempt to kill Machmud himself, and possibly Surabaya, that PLA was becoming more aggressive in their efforts to complete their death list, and that therefore my time was running short. If Machmud had gotten into that limousine on the previous night, my work against PLA, no matter how successful, would have seemed pretty anti-climactic.

It was 8.17 when I sat down across the small table at the coffee-house on Madjahapit Street. Sarasin was on his way to work, and looked wan and weary. He was a slight man with big almond eyes and balding hair. He always wore a haunted look on his narrow face.

'Do you have anything else for me, Sarasin?' I asked him after we had been served the thick black coffee I had ordered for us.

He nodded, glancing around us. There was nobody nearby. 'He goes to the Sembilan Bar this noon, for a sandwich and beer,' Sarasin said. 'He ought to be coming out of the place at about one.'

'Will he be alone?' I said.

He shrugged. 'He did not say. I overheard him speaking with a subordinate.'

I sat there thinking. It sounded good.

'There is an empty building directly across the street, Mr Smith,' Sarasin told me. 'With a clear view of the front entrance of the Sembilan Bar.'

I nodded my understanding. I took some rupiahs out of my pocket, counted off a generous sum, and handed it to him under the table. He took it. I rose and swigged the rest of the coffee.

'Thanks,' I said. 'Keep on it,' I added non-commitally.

Sarasin nodded, and I left.

Back at my small headquarters in the closed-down building, in the dormitory room, Batak was just finishing cleaning up from his breakfast, and Chaban was propped on a cot with a cup of coffee, reading a Paris newspaper he had purchased the previous evening. He was still smoldering over our encounter in the alleyway, and was speaking to neither myself nor Batak unless he was spoken to. He looked up balefully when I entered, then went back to reading the paper.

Batak nodded to me. 'Did you find him, Rainey?' He was dressed in a light-colored tropical worsted suit now, too, like Chaban and I wore. He did not want to announce to the world that he was in the Presidential Guard.

'I found him,' I said. 'Would the two of you come on over here while we go over this?'

Batak dropped a dish towel, came over and seated himself at the table. Chaban put the paper down, gave me a hard look, and slowly rose from the cot and stretched, to show his boredom with all this. He walked over and leaned on the table, while I sat down and began sketching a drawing of the street the bar was on.

'Rainey,' he said with sarcasm, 'it seems to me that you much prefer drawing maps and having meetings than actually liquidating our enemies.'

I gave him a look.

'When do you intend to go out and really kill somebody, Rainey?' he demanded.

'How would one o'clock suit you?' I said acidly. 'Do you think you can last until then, Chaban?'

'One o'clock in the afternoon?' he said. 'Today?'

'That's right,' I told him.

His face changed subtly, and he sat down slowly at the table and glanced at my drawing.

Batak rubbed a muscular hand across his chin. 'When you move, Rainey,' he said, 'you move.'

'The time is right,' I told them. 'At noon today, Malik will be at the Sembilan Bar. He's going to have a quick lunch there. At about one, he'll come out the front entrance to return to his office. We'll be out there waiting for him.'

'Will he be alone?' Chaban asked.

'I don't know. I suppose he might be meeting someone. But unless it's another of our five targets, we hit only Malik. Understood?'

Chaban shrugged. Batak nodded his agreement.

'This building here,' I said, pointing to the drawing with a pencil, 'is empty, and gives a full view of the entrance of the Sembilan Bar. Batak, you'll be in a third-story window, with a sniper rifle, and you'll make the hit.'

Chaban looked up at me, his face dark with angry surprise. 'Why not me?' he said evenly. 'Why not me with the rifle? What the hell are you trying to prove, Rainey?'

I turned to him. 'Not a damned thing,' I said. 'I don't have the time or energy to fight with you through this, Chaban. Our methodology dictates who uses the gun this time. I know you know more ways to kill than either Batak or I. But this frontal assault requires excellence with a rifle. Batak is the best there is. His military record shows it. Therefore he makes the kill this time. You and I will be on the ground, as back-up only.'

'Back-up!' Chaban snorted, turning away.

Batak and I exchanged glances. I kept on then, as if Chaban had not interrupted. 'Chaban will be directly across the street on ground level, inside the doorway of a closed shop in the same building.' Chaban turned back to watch me place him on the paper, his curiosity getting the better of him. 'I'll be here,' I pointed, 'leaning on our stolen car. Neither Chaban nor I will do any shooting unless something goes wrong on your end, Batak. You'll stay inside the building, though, even if you have to back Batak up, Chaban. Under no circumstances will you emerge onto the street, even to keep Malik from escaping alive.'

Chaban grunted.

'Under no circumstances, also, will there be any shooting of any person except Malik, or another of our targets in PLA.' I was looking directly at Chaban. 'Except in defense of our lives.'

'Do you want a brain shot,' Batak asked seriously, 'or shall I go for the heart?'

I turned to him. All of this was new to me. It was as if we were discussing hunting Cape buffalo in East Africa.

'I'm going to leave that to your discretion, Batak,' I told him. 'If there is any doubt about your ability to hit your target, take the bigger one – his chest. Don't hesitate to shoot more than once. As soon as you're through firing, leave. You won't be taking the rifle. I want you to wear silk gloves and leave your equipment.' I turned to Chaban. 'Do you want to improve on that, Chaban?'

Chaban laughed a hard laugh in his throat. 'As a matter of fact, I do,' he said bitterly. 'Malik should make an easy target, so I think Batak should be instructed to go for the head first, under any circumstance. He can always fire again, for a larger target area, if something goes wrong. But if he hits the head on the first try, it's over.'

I looked over to Batak.

'I shall give that my consideration,' Batak said stiffly.

'Also, there is a tendency to overshoot at a lower-level target,' Chaban went on. 'Your sight should be compensated for this factor.'

'I am aware of this,' Batak said.

'A last point I would make is that this is not a target range we are going to,' Chaban said. 'I don't know how much big-game hunting you have done, Captain, but this is what we will be doing. You must wait for a favorable shot, and you must ignore everything around your target, no matter how much else is happening. Probably most important is that you have the killer instinct – that you think of yourself as a predator. Do you have that feeling, Captain?'

Batak glared at him. 'I'll do the job, Chaban.'

I wondered how this mission was going to come out, with the three of us trying to operate together. We discussed a few more details about the part that was to come off shortly, and then we prepared to leave for the Sembilan Bar.

We were situated at 11.45. I had checked at 11.40 and found that Malik had just arrived. He was with another man, but I was not able to find out who the companion was without arousing undue curiosity inside. So we situated ourselves and waited.

Chaban had stolen a car for us just before we arrived, a small Citroen, and I now stood at the car across the street from the entrance to the bar. We would return the car after the action against Malik. Batak was in a window overlooking the street, in the closed-down building. I could just get a glimpse of him up there, from my position. The window was raised about six inches, to give him an uncluttered view.

Chaban and I had Malik flanked on ground level, when he came out. I was about twenty feet down the street from the bar entrance, and Chaban was down the other way, in the shop entrance behind a partially-closed door.

Chaban was not using his Mauser for this operation. With my permission, he had brought a Belgian Centennial .44 revolver with an eight-inch barrel and a detachable carbine stock. It was powerful, and almost as accurate as a rifle, yet easy to take with him when we left. I was depending on my Star .45, the stubby automatic that had kept me out of trouble so many times in the past.

I flashed a message to Batak and Chaban that there was someone with Malik, and then I leaned on the Citroen, on the street side, facing the bar, and smoked a cigarette. It got to be 12.15, then 12.45.

I knew it would not be long now. Unfortunately, there was a lot more activity in the street than I had imagined there would be. Pedestrian traffic was steady, and an occasional car or bike would pass by. A policeman came down the street at 12.50, looked into the bar, and sauntered on down the street a small distance and stepped into a small shop there. I breathed again.

At 1.05, Malik showed.

He was not alone.

Ibn Solkar, the Deputy Police Commissioner, was with him. Solkar was another of the PLA leaders on our death list.

I caught my breath. It could be good luck, or bad, according to how we handled it. If Batak kept his cool, recognized Solkar, and placed his shots well, he could probably get both of them. I would jump into the Citroen, pick up Chaban down the street, drive around the block and get Batak on his way out of the rear side of the building he was shooting from.

But it seems that things never go exactly the way you plan them.

While I was still running through all that in my mind, Batak's first shot rang out, as Malik and Solkar stood talking on the sidewalk for a moment outside the door. Malik, a stout, very oriental-looking man, suddenly jumped sidewise as the rifle barked out above me. Bone and matter sprayed from the hole on the far side of his head, and crimson spattered onto Solkar's neat suit.

Malik hit the pavement dead, and it was very messy. Solkar just stood there for a long moment, stunned, while Chaban and I waited for the other shot to ring out. It finally did, just as Solkar turned to run down the street.

The rifle shot hit Solkar in the side, and slammed him up against a building wall. A couple of women near him screamed, and other pedestrians were running for cover. Solkar did not go down. Before Batak could fire again, Chaban came storming out of his cover, swearing, dropped into a low crouch and fired at Solkar three times in rapid succession, the Centennial stock against his shoulder. The tall, rangy Solkar jumped and jerked against the building wall, hit in the abdomen, the chest, and the neck. He stared glassy-eyed toward Chaban for a moment, then slid to the pavement, leaving blood on the wall behind him. There was little doubt that Chaban had killed him.

Now, however, the policeman who had turned into the small shop came storming back out, his pistol drawn, his eyes wild as he spotted his big boss Solkar lying bloody and lifeless on the sidewalk.

I jumped into the Citroen, swearing, and started its engine. 'Damn it, let's go!' I yelled at Chaban, who was near the car, out in full view of the pedestrians and the cop.

Chaban had seen the policeman, though, and when the cop raised his pistol toward Chaban and yelled for him to disarm himself, Chaban coolly fired the Centennial twice more, hitting the policeman in the chest twice. The policeman was punched off his feet with two holes in him, and lay rolling in agony on the pavement.

I drove up beside Chaban, he piled into the car, and I burned rubber and roared away. A woman pedestrian almost got in the way of the car as I squealed around her and then skidded around a corner.

By the time I got around to the far side of the block, Batak was there. I slowed down, he piled in and we hurtled off into the afternoon heat, with a couple of pedestrians staring hard after us. I zig-zagged around a few more blocks until we came to a narrow side street, and pulled to a stop there where there were no witnesses. We abandoned the Citroen, one by one, and walked around a corner to the Fiat. Batak had donned a gay print shirt over his black sweater, and Chaban had removed his suit jacket, so they would present a different appearance. In just a couple of minutes we had changed cars and I drove the Fiat away, heading for our headquarters. Off in another direction, we could hear the klaxons of police cars, rushing to the Sembilan Bar.

When we got onto a slow-trafficked street and could relax some, Batak said to Chaban, 'Why did you shoot?'

Chaban was his usual arrogant self. 'Because you failed to,' he said harshly.

Batak was in the back seat, and Chaban was sitting up beside me. I turned to him briefly. I was very angry. 'Goddam it, Chaban. You didn't give him a chance. There must be twenty witnesses to your shooting of Solkar. And you went against my specific orders and shot that cop.'

Chaban shrugged. 'He had a gun. He might have killed one of us.'

We both knew, though, that we could probably have escaped without a shoot-out with the cop. Chaban had wanted the confrontation. He had been geared up to kill.

I stared ahead, guiding the car through light traffic. We were almost back at our headquarters now. 'You enjoy it too goddam much, Chaban. You disobeyed orders, and brought attention to yourself and to me. If I had just a little time to replace you, I'd fire you in a minute.'

Chaban was very self-satisfied. 'I killed one of the five men we have set out to liquidate. I would have gotten both of them with no commotion, if you had let me handle it.'

We turned a corner, and I pulled up to the curb. Our annex headquarters was just down the street. I sighed heavily, and turned to Chaban. My anger had already been tempered by the thought of our double-strike success. There were only three PLA killers left, now. And Rublev.

'You're still on the team for the moment,' I told Chaban. 'But I want you to know where you stand with me, in the meantime. I see you as a soulless bastard who enjoys killing for the pleasure he gets out of it. A sonofabitch who would take a contract on his own mother for the ego trip it would give him.'

Chaban could not be upset, though. He had, in his mind, showed up both Batak and me in his grandstand display of gunplay at the shoot-out. 'Well, Rainey,' he said suavely, grinning his hard grin at me, 'nobody is perfect.'

Six

Malik and Solkar, as I had suspected, were dead when they hit the pavement. The policeman who intervened died that evening at a local hospital, and Chaban had already killed, in my opinion, unnecessarily.

I went to a phone that evening and called a special number and got President Machmud on the other end. I reported our success, which he had already heard about through the police. He was exuberant, and I knew he wondered why I was not. I did not feel like discussing Chaban with him just then, though. I stopped at a small bar on the way back to the annex building, a place I had frequented in the past in an old part of town, and found Nellie Ullah there. She was sitting at the bar, showing a great deal of her long legs. I took a stool beside her, and she was delighted to see me.

'What made you come here?' I asked her.

She was wearing a green sheath dress, a short one, with green heels and accessories. Her long dark hair really set it off. She looked particularly appealing.

'Because,' she explained, 'I knew I might see you here.'

I grinned. 'That's nice.'

She let me order her a drink. A juke-box was going, and a sailor came over and asked her to dance, and she declined. The way the sailor looked at her made me want her even more than I already did.

'I heard about the shootings,' she finally said, when we were alone. 'Should I congratulate you?'

'Nellie!' I warned her.

'I know, you know nothing about the assassination of these known leftists. But I think, Jim, that these men are involved in the recent killings, and that you are here to do something about it. You need not admit that to me, of course.'

'I strongly suggest you forget all about what's going on around you in Djakarta, until it's all over,' I said seriously.

'Oh, I will, lover,' she smiled. 'But I thought I would mention something I've learned about Ahmad Rahimat, the leftist lawyer.'

'What makes you think I would have any interest in Rahimat?' I said, marveling at her insight.

'Oh, you would have none, of course. This is just a matter I thought I would mention in passing. Rahimat has called President Machmud personally, the rumor says, and has accused him of being involved in these killings, saying Machmud has hired the CIA to get rid of all of his political opponents. Do you suppose that means Rahimat is one of the persons responsible for the assassinations, and that these deaths today – which you had nothing to do with, naturally – are making him nervous?'

I gave the bartender a wad of rupiahs, and asked him if I might make use of the privacy of a back room I had been in on previous occasions. He took the money, and I guided Nellie into the room, under the knowing look of the bartender, and also the sailor who had approached her earlier. I turned a small-bulb light on, and locked the door behind us.

The room was spartan, with a table and chairs where customers sometimes played cards, and a cot on one wall. There was an unopened bottle of brandy on the table, and a couple of glasses. But I had not brought Nellie in here to ply her with liquor.

I turned her to me. She looked delicious. 'Listen,' I said, 'don't you know that you can't talk of such matters in public? It's dangerous, Nellie.'

She reached up to my lips with hers and kissed me. She tasted damn good.

'Okay, Jim. Whatever you say. I just wanted you to know of Rahimat's nervousness. In case you didn't know. He is supposedly taking a weekend trip to his cottage near Palembang, probably to get his nerve back.'

I tuned in suddenly. I had known that Rahimat had a place near Palembang, on the neighboring island of Sumatra. In fact, it was suspected that the PLA five had met there – probably with the KGB man Rublev – to plan this current rash of assassinations of top political and military leaders. But Rahimat had apparently not been back there since that time, and we would not have looked for him there. It occurred to me that this might not be a bad place to make our move against him, since the cottage was remote and lonely, and Rahimat would probably be pretty much alone there.

Nellie was kissing me again, and making me forget what I had in mind for Rahimat. My hands found her curves of their own volition, it seemed, and then her fragile hand was inside my suit trousers. All the while she was kissing me hungrily. She was some woman, and I was glad I had not missed seeing her while I was in Djakarta. Now the trousers were unzipped, and Nellie was finding what she had been going after. It was all very subtly done, and innocuous, but suddenly there I was, ready for her.

I reached up over my head and pulled the light off, and we were standing in a darkness broken only by a bar of dim light from a high window on the far wall. I had Nellie's green sheath up around her hips now, and as before, there was no cloth between her and me once the dress was raised. We effected a union while still standing under the swinging, dark bulb, and Nellie's gasp filled the small room.

'The cot,' she breathed, as we moved together.

I don't know how we got onto it. I was thinking of how much that hungry sailor out in the bar would like to have been in my place at that very moment, and that stoked my fire even higher. It should have been irrelevant, but it wasn't.

Also, I had thought that that last episode at Nellie's place had dampened the flame that had burned inside me for three years for Nellie, but I was wrong. I was obviously still releasing a deep-down frustration that had pleasantly tormented me all that time. In the next few minutes, the cot shook with our gyrations, and Nellie's throaty cries filled the dark room. I drank of nectar for the gods in that cramped, airless place in the back of that Djakarta bar.

When it was over, I had forgotten why I brought Nellie in there. My lecture to her about Rahimat seemed to have taken place a thousand years ago. We sat up on the cot and I lit up a cigarette, took a long drag on it, and passed if over to her. She put it between her full lips and closed her eyes and remembered. No matter what she did, she was beautiful.

'I have to go,' I finally said.

'I knew you would.'

'I'm glad you found me, Nellie.'

'Me, too.'

'Don't do it again.'

She looked at me.

'It's much too dangerous,' I said. 'I'm too dangerous.'

She nodded.

'I'll get you a cab.'

When I got back to the dormitory room, only Chaban was there. Batak had gone out to a nearby café for a beer. Chaban was busy cleaning the Belgian Centennial he had used with such deadly efficiency earlier in the day. We mumbled greetings to each other, and I sat down at the table in the center of the room.

Chaban glanced up at me, from his cot over on the wall, to my left. 'I think we should hit Quan next,' he said.

I regarded him impassively. 'Oh?'

'Once Quan is dead, the others will panic. It will be merely a clean-up operation from that point on.'

'What about the Russian?'

Chaban had had no experience with intelligence people, so had no respect for them. 'Ahh!' he said, making a face. 'Russian spies are a dime a dozen, as you Americans say. He will run to Moscow like a rabbit when he realizes what is happening to his new friends. He may be gone already.'

'You don't give him much,' I said.

He shrugged. 'Anyway, I say Quan must be next.'

I shook my head. 'I just got some information on Rahimat. He's going to his Sumatra cottage this weekend. Maybe alone. That would be a good place to catch him.'

Chaban made another face. 'The lawyer? *Mon dieu*, Rainey, must you persist in picking the easy targets first? Are you afraid to go after Quan or Afandi?'

'Are you afraid to proceed by a logical plan, rather than waving your gun wildly in all directions?' I said harshly. 'Deep down, Chaban, are you afraid you're not a man, if you're not firing that Mauser off every hour on the hour?'

Chaban stopped cleaning the Centennial. His face had gone very hard. His handsomeness left when he looked like this, and was replaced by a violent ugliness. 'You think you speak to Michel Chaban like this, because you have been placed in authority here temporarily!' He had finished cleaning and re-loading the long pistol, and it now dangled loosely in his right hand.

'I'd tell you what I thought of you if I was only sweeping the floors here,' I told him deliberately. 'It's Rahimat next, Chaban, and not because I have any reluctance to go after the big politico Quan with his new bodyguards, or Colonel Afandi surrounded by his military. It's because it's right to hit Rahimat now. We'll fly to Palembang tomorrow. And I've just made a new rule.'

I rose from the chair. 'Weapons will be stashed until we're ready to move. All through the operation.'

Chaban stared at me as if I had lost my mind. Then a laugh began deep in his throat, and exploded into the room. He had a good one. Finally, he spoke, 'Do you really think I will turn over my weaponry to you, Rainey?' he said. 'I am never without my little arsenal. And it has nothing to do with what I think of myself as a man. I have learned that to be armed is to survive.' He stood up beside the cot, and turned the Centennial over in his hand. 'I do not intend to change my ways now.'

There was a sudden tension crackling through the room. It was our second showdown. I could not help but wonder whether I had started something I could not finish. But I had made up my mind on the way back here. Chaban was too gun-happy to be armed all the time. He made me damned uncomfortable.

I walked over to Chaban, and when I got there, I saw that the loaded Centennial was aimed approximately at my groin. Chaban was also wearing the Mauser in a shoulder holster over his shirt. I stopped just a few feet from him, and he grinned a hard grin.

'Are you going to disarm me, Rainey?'

'I'll take the Centennial first,' I said grimly.

'Go to hell,' he told me.

In the next instant I grabbed the muzzle of the Centennial.

It was a tactic that every good soldier knew, designed to disarm an enemy who has taken you captive. In a split-second I shoved the muzzle to my left and stepped to my right, turning my back to Chaban as I stepped into him.

The gun went off loudly beside me, tearing at my suit jacket at my side, and then I had Chaban's gun hand in a double grip. I twisted hard and the gun was flung from his grasp, across the room. I felt a punch to my low back and hissed in pain. Then I bent forward, still clutching Chaban's right hand, and pulled hard. Chaban came flying over my head and shoulder, and banged hard on the floor on his back, in front of me. I could hear the air punched from his lungs when he hit. He was stunned for a moment, and in that instant I reached and pulled the Mauser from his shoulder holster and threw it away from us.

Chaban scrambled to his knee, and then to his feet, as I rose also, still hurting from the punch he had landed. He was raging furious now. He mumbled an obscenity in French, and threw a hard punch at my face.

I ducked aside and it still grazed my jaw and jarred me. Chaban was good with his hands, as well as with weapons. I jammed a right in under his defenses and caught him in the belly, low, and he was breathing hard again. He kicked out at my groin and just missed, landing a hard blow on my upper thigh. I grabbed the foot and pulled, and Chaban hit violently on his back for the second time.

This time he did not get up so fast. When he did, I was there waiting. I threw a hard punch into his face this time, and heard bone snap in his nose. He staggered backwards several steps, lost his balance, and went down for good.

He just lay there then, glaring up at me through blurred vision, I guessed, and a bloody face. I saw a hatred in that look at that moment that was not a little unnerving.

'Now,' I said breathlessly. 'If you want out, get out of here. But if you stay, you stay by my rules.'

I thought he would leave. But apparently the money was more than Chaban had made in some time. He sat up and put a hand to his mouth. 'You have made a foolish mistake, Rainey,' he growled. 'You have made an enemy of me.'

'Does that mean you're pulling out?'

He sat there a moment, then got up unsteadily and went to sit on the edge of his cot. 'No, you will not deprive me of my payment that easily,' he said.

I went and retrieved his two guns, while he continued.

'But, some time before this is over, Rainey,' he went on, 'there will be a reckoning. I will kill you. You can count on it.'

I looked over at Chaban and saw his deadly grim face, and knew he was very serious. I had been right about him – the man was all twisted up inside. I know I should fire him right there, or kill him, maybe. But killing in cold blood was not my style. And I needed Chaban, if I was to finish the job I set out to do.

'You'd better let it go, Chaban,' I said as I locked his guns into a small chest in a corner of the room. I turned back to him. 'That's fair warning.'

He grinned the harsh grin again, and I knew why. If he really wanted to kill me before our job was through, there was damned little I could do to stop him.

And we both knew it.

Seven

The following day, the account of the killing of Malik and Solkar was in all the newspapers. It was also on the lips of every man in the street, and conjecture was rampant.

We knew now that Quan would guess that Machmud had organized a counter-plot against PLA. Rahimat had already harangued Machmud by phone, accusing him of hiring CIA assassins to 'wipe out' his political opposition. Machmud had feigned ignorance of both the counter-plot and the PLA plot, to keep PLA guessing as long as possible.

Ali Quan was seen that very morning with three bodyguards in attendance, whom he was referring to as 'business associates'. Colonel Nur Afandi, the tough military man of the leaders, was keeping pretty much on his base, surrounded by his soldiers, in a camp near Djakarta. The lawyer Rahimat had disappeared from town, and I figured he had already taken off for his cottage near Palembang until things cooled off some.

I went to Machmud early that morning, leaving the disarmed Chaban and Batak at our small headquarters. Batak had surrendered his gun willingly, and had very much enjoyed my disarming the arrogant and dangerous Chaban. They were not speaking at all to each other, and I could only guess at the ways they found to avoid each other when I left them alone in those closer quarters.

I met Machmud at the Guard headquarters at ten, and Surabaya joined us at almost 10.30. Both of them were very congratulatory, and for the first time since the Quan-led plot began, they were just a little optimistic about their own personal survival.

'We can't tell you how pleased we are with this dramatic

beginning, Rainey,' Surabaya told me, his square face full of excitement.

'You should have heard Rahimat,' Machmud offered, smiling. 'It is pleasant seeing them go on the defensive. I hope they don't become so cautious that your job becomes more difficult.' He was wearing a plain suit and tie, and had begun wearing his prescription sunglasses in preference to his wire spectacles, whenever he went out. He looked very political.

'That's a danger, of course,' I acknowledged.

'Now what?' Machmud asked. 'Do we move against Colonel Afandi, perhaps? There is information that he is coming into town tomorrow. Perhaps it is to confer with Ali Quan.'

I had made up my mind. I was going to be cagey about what I planned next. The more people knew, the more danger there was to the operation.

'I don't really know what's our next good move,' I replied to Machmud. 'I'll look into the possibility of going after Afandi. I doubt he'll take any risks, though, in the next few days. Even to confer with Quan.'

Machmud seemed disappointed by my answer. 'I see,' he said.

'I'm going to have to coalesce all our intelligence, and then decide what's best for us,' I hedged. 'I'll be in touch with you further, of course, as we go along in this. But I'll have to recommend that we meet less frequently. It's too dangerous for you personally, and for the operation.'

Surabaya had suggested the meeting, and he now looked somber after my suggestion. 'We need close communication, though, Rainey,' he said. 'We come by information daily that can help you.'

'I know,' I said. 'I'll call you once every twenty-four hours, just for that reason. You'll be our central intelligence source. As for meetings – '

There was a knock on the door. We had never been disturbed in a meeting before, because so few persons knew of it. Surabaya opened the door, and a major stood there. He spoke to Surabaya briefly in subdued tones, then disappeared. Surabaya closed the door and turned back to us, his face grave.

'PLA has retaliated already,' he said heavily. 'Another person on their death list has been killed – General Nahdatul.'

'Damn!' Machmud muttered.

I sighed heavily.

'It was apparently pretty bloody,' Surabaya said quietly. 'He was decapitated with some kind of sharp instrument.'

'They want to scare you,' I said.

Machmud grunted. 'They have.'

'This just makes it all the more clear,' I said, 'that we have no time to waste. Any delay can cost us another life, and we never know whose.'

Machmud glanced toward me, and he no longer had the bright look on his face he had worn when we started the meeting.

'End it, Rainey,' he said firmly. 'End it quickly before it is too late for us.'

I held his somber gaze. 'I'll do my best, Mr President,' I told him.

Machmud let out a long breath. 'I sincerely hope that your best is good enough,' he commented.

Sumatra is much more primitive than the island of Java, where Djakarta is located. Most of the island is jungle, and there are still a lot of wild animals around. Monkeys chatter in the trees and big snakes slither underfoot and elephants roam the wilds, with the natives trying to keep out of their way. Batak and I knew all this before we flew to Palembang, but I think it came as quite a surprise to Chaban, who was a city man.

I got us tickets for an early afternoon flight, and we were in Palembang by two. The airport was hot and humid, and the rented car we picked up there was small and uncomfortable. Chaban grumbled about it a lot, and that seemed to make Batak tolerate it all more easily.

Palembang is a small town compared with Djakarta. It has a couple of main streets downtown where there are hotels and shops, but mostly it is pretty primitive. The Dutch Colonial buildings in the central area give away quickly to corrugated-iron shanties and primitive huts, and you are always aware that the jungle is not far away, just at the edge of the town. You have to be careful what restaurants you eat in, and where you take a room. Lice and rats are common at many local establishments, in addition to other colorful pests.

We had gotten the location of Rahimat's cottage near Palembang before we left Djakarta, so we did not stay in town longer than to grab a quick meal at the best restaurant we could find. Within an hour of our arrival at the airport, we were under way from Palembang, heading out into the bush.

The road was narrow. It was paved for only a mile or so, and then it was dirt. Exotic palms, banana trees and other tropical foliage crowded in on us as we drove. In an occasional open field we saw straw-hatted women planting rice. One such field crew was using an elephant to haul a pallet of rice seedlings. As we got deeper into the bush, we began hearing the yelling of monkeys and raucous birds.

Batak rode up front with me. Chaban sulked in the rear, looking dangerous. I kept thinking, driving along that backwoods road, that this was a perfect time for him to draw the Mauser that he now wore in the open over khakis, as we all did, and shoot me in the back of the head. I would not have put it past him. He was a dark, crazy person inside, and I knew I would have more trouble with him before this was all over.

I had toyed with the idea of trying to get along with him on this jaunt to Sumatra. Rahimat did not appear to be one of our difficult prey. But you just never knew for sure. You did not take extra chances because you did not like being around somebody. So Chaban was with us.

We drove for almost an hour, and finally came to a small village. It was really primitive. Thatched huts made up most of the buildings there. Dirty children played in the dust, and pet monkeys swung from hut poles. Behind the huts were small fields of grain, probably rice. Back in the jungle somewhere, I had been told, was the ruins of an old temple of some kind. But we were not there to explore the archaeological heritage of the area. We had come to kill.

Rahimat's cottage was supposedly less than a mile from the village, which was called Manokwari. We drove most of that distance in first gear, over rutted roads, and came to a turn-off, a kind of private drive.

I pulled the car over onto a pull-off beside the drive, and stopped it under a tree where it was surrounded by lush greenery.

A tropical bird called out loudly nearby, making Chaban swing his head around quickly.

'*Mon Dieu!*' he grumbled, surveying our wild surroundings.

'The real Indonesia,' Batak said to himself.

Off to our right, a group of monkeys chattered loudly in a treetop. I climbed out of the car and looked down the narrow, overgrown drive, and saw nothing. It curved away from view about thirty yards into the jungle, where vines and lianas crowded in on it uncomfortably.

'Okay,' I said.

Batak climbed out. He looked tough in his khakis, with the service revolver on his hip. Chaban got out warily, the Mauser 7.65 stuck in his belt instead of in a holster. I was wearing my shoulder holster over the khakis, with the Star .45 tucked in its usual place under my left arm.

'Batak, head on up the drive,' I said, 'on its left side. Carefully. You follow on the right, Chaban, about ten yards behind. I'll bring up the rear.'

Batak nodded and moved out. Chaban moved past me and grinned. 'What is the matter, Rainey? You don't want me behind you, *oui*?'

'Get moving, Chaban,' I said curtly. 'And try not to let them see you coming.'

I said 'them' because I figured Rahimat would at least have a servant or two with him at the cottage. I hoped it was not more than that.

We moved carefully along the drive, branches and fronds brushing at our faces and clothing. A big tarantula crawled around the other side of a banana tree as I passed, hiding from us. Further along, Chaban almost stepped on a small green snake that I could not identify, but which was probably dangerous. I found myself almost wishing he had not seen it. We turned the curve in the drive, and Chaban caught up with Batak.

'*Depechez-vous!*' he whispered harshly to Batak, hurrying him along.

Batak gave him a hard look. '*Ati ati!*' he hissed back at Chaban '*Moendoer!*' telling Chaban to keep back.

In another twenty yards we came to the cottage. It sat in the center of a rough clearing about fifty yards in diameter. There was a lawn of sorts, but it was weed-grown. The house had a thatch roof and reed-and-bamboo walls, and fit into its surroundings very aesthetically. For some illogical reason, it bothered me that Rahimat might have aesthetic sensibility. There was a porch around to the far side that was screened. All the windows were open and also screened. The mosquitoes that now buzzed around us told us why. Beside the house was a Mercedes-Benz 200-SL, green in color. The bastard even had good taste in automobiles.

From inside the cottage came the sound of a radio on. There was music playing, a modernized oriental folk music. Batak turned to me and nodded, meaning that Rahimat was probably there. I nodded my agreement. Chaban grunted.

I gestured for them to get down, to crawl in on the cottage in the tall grass and weeds. We would be perfectly camouflaged in the brown foliage of the lawn. Chaban looked at me as if I was playing soldier again. I gave him a second gesture, a tougher one, and he got down reluctantly. Batak and he began crawling up toward the cottage according to previous plan – Batak toward the front porch of the place, and Chaban toward a rear door near the Mercedes.

I waited back at the edge of the clearing. I wished I had brought binoculars, to see better. There was no way of knowing whether Rahimat had brought protection with him. There was probably plenty available yet, despite our killing of a couple of the gunmen. They had hired a number of them, right in Palembang, not long ago.

When Batak reached the house, I started out. I got down and crawled through the grass and weeds, keeping my head low. If anybody looked outside, he might see us anyway, but the chances were reduced. I glanced off to my right, and saw that Chaban had gotten up onto his knees, tired of crawling. That was the trouble with having someone along who had never had formal military training. He might be a flawless killer, but he knew almost nothing about tactics.

I swore under my breath, hoping he would turn so I could wave him down. Batak was within fifteen feet of the front porch now, and dangerously exposed. But Chaban did not look back. I was just about to make an audible signal to him – an attempt to emulate a bird call – when the rear door of the cottage suddenly swung open and the brawny man emerged.

Instead of freezing in position, Chaban now dropped down from the low crouch he had assumed, to his belly.

The brawny man saw the movement.

In the next instant he yelled something in Indonesian and went for a gun in his belt. Chaban responded by drawing down on him with the Mauser, and firing.

The gunman, obviously some kind of bodyguard for Rahimat, yelled again after the explosion from Chaban's gun, as he was hit high in the chest. He was punched off his feet and hit the ground beside the doorway he had just come through.

'Damn!' I muttered.

Batak was up near the front porch, in almost no cover. There was the sound of at least two men's voices from inside, and then another gunman stormed outside from the porch, almost on top of Batak, gun drawn. He saw Batak immediately and fired three shots at him, at point-blank range.

The first shot missed Batak, but the second one hit him in the chest as he rose to defend himself, just over the heart. He was thrown onto his side, and it was there that the third slug caught him in the face, exploding into his skull. I saw him jump and jerk on the ground for a moment, and that was it.

I swore again, bitterly, got down on one knee and aimed the Star with both hands. The gunman saw both Chaban and me, and chose me as his next target. I saw the big gun swing toward me as I squeezed twice on the trigger.

The Star banged out in the clearing two times, and the gunman was slammed against the screen of the porch, tearing it open, and then punched on through it. Both slugs had hit him in center chest.

We had run into unexpected opposition. Rahimat had brought gunmen with him after all. Now, because of Chaban's stupidity, Batak was dead, and we still did not have Rahimat.

I rose to my feet, and waved at Chaban angrily. '*Go on in!*' I yelled at him. '*Now, damn it!*'

Chaban gave me a look, then headed up to the cottage. He should have run like hell, to get to cover of the building as quickly as possible, but he went carefully. I was boiling inside, but there was no time for anger. I raced to the front porch, past Batak, who was lying in a widening pool of blood, lifeless, his eyes still wide open. The slug that killed him had entered through his left cheek and ripped through his head and punched a hole in the back of his skull.

I came on past the dead gunman, who actually lay inside on the porch. He was very dead. I went around to a screen door, and it was wide open. I went through it and crossed the porch with its bamboo lawn furniture to an inner doorway. I could hear voices inside. At least one other man was there with Rahimat.

Just as I glanced inside, I heard a shot out the back. I figured someone was firing at Chaban, and I almost hoped they had hit him. Then I heard his return fire.

I moved quickly into a rather spacious living room, and then out of the light from the door. There was nobody in there. Sunlight came softly into the room through louvered shutters on several windows. There was more primitive furniture, and a potted palm. A spilled drink lay on the tiled floor.

There were more shots out back. I hurried to an archway to the kitchen and saw a short native wearing an apron. He was apparently Rahimat's servant, probably the only one left alive except for Rahimat. He had found a gun and was firing at Chaban from a rear window, faced away from me.

'Surprise!' I said to him.

He turned quickly, gun in hand. I fired the Star just once, and hit him in the middle chest. He fell back over a counter where dishes were stacked, and brought them all down with him as he fell to the floor. While that was going on, I slipped down a corridor to a couple of bedrooms.

I glanced in the first room and saw nothing. Everything was quiet in there. I moved past the doorway. Then I heard the almost inaudible sound behind me. I got just a glimpse of the knife blade as it plunged at my ribs.

Twisting desperately away, I tried to reach for the blade with my free left hand, but missed and got a cut on my left forearm as the knife was shoved at my side. The twisting movement spoiled my assailant's aim, though. The knife ripped through my khaki shirt in a long slash, but only nicked my flesh underneath. I swung on around with the Star, to smash it into his face, but he was further to my rear than I had guessed, and my hand banged into the door jamb beside him and knocked the Star from my grasp.

I fell off-balance against the wall, and saw my assailant for the first time. I had seen that face once before, with its hard, intelligent eyes and slim, strong jaw. We had met in that corridor at the Presidential Guard headquarters. It was Ahmad Rahimat.

He hesitated only briefly as he came in with the knife again. 'You!' he hissed. Then he shoved the knife again at my body, this time going for the abdomen.

I caught the knife hand this time, though, and held it at bay. Rahimat's arm trembled with the effort to drive it home. In a brief moment I got my other hand onto his wrist, and was twisting. There was a cracking sound, and Rahimat yelled loudly as bone snapped. The knife clattered to the floor. I jammed stiffened fingers into his throat, and he yelled again and fell onto his back on the floor, gagging violently. I found the Star near me, picked it up, and aimed it at Rahimat's chest.

'No!' he gasped, choking. 'Don't kill me! I was a – dupe. It was Quan's and Afandi's – idea. Please.'

I hesitated a brief moment, hating to kill a man in cold blood, but knowing I had to do it. In that brief second, Chaban came storming into the corridor, saw Rahimat begging for his life, and aimed and fired the Mauser at him twice.

The shots hit Rahimat in center chest, both of them. He jumped on the floor with both of them, and then his leg kicked at the floor once, and he was dead.

Chaban looked over at me coldly. I thought for a moment he was going to use a third bullet on me. 'Is that all of them?' he said. There was no concern for the dead Batak, no emotion at all, it seemed.

I did not answer him. I was too charged with emotion myself. I brushed past him, hitting his shoulder as I went, knocking him aside. I kept the Star in hand in case he should change his mind about me when I turned my back on him. I went out to the porch and he followed me out there. I examined the gunman who had punched a hole in the screen with his body, and made sure he was dead. Then I went outside and bent over Batak. I just knelt there for a long moment, then I took everything from his pockets and crammed it into mine.

Chaban came up beside me. 'Hmmph. Too bad about the wog,' he said in his French accent.

I turned to him. I wondered if I should just kill him and leave him there at the cottage. But that was not my style.

'You killed him,' I said, 'with stupidity.'

His face darkened. 'Now, look, Rainey – '

'To hell with that,' I growled. 'The talking is over. I won't work with you any more, Chaban. You're fired, as far as I'm concerned. If that means this is a good time for you to make your try for me, go ahead.'

We stood there facing each other over Batak. Both of us were still armed, the guns hanging at our sides, ready for use. I was telling Chaban, in my way, that if he wanted to kill me, now was the time to do it, like a man.

Finally he spoke. 'No, Rainey. I think I would prefer to see you explain to Machmud how I'm no longer a part of your team. With Batak dead, that should be an interesting announcement to him. I would guess it will meet with little favor, Rainey. In fact, I just might end up running this thing after all.' He let a tight grin move his hard face.

I did not reply to him. 'See you back at the car, Chaban,' I told him.

Then I turned and headed back across the hot, fly-buzzing clearing toward the jungle.

Eight

There was no communication between Chaban and me all the way back to Palembang, and we took seats apart on the plane back to Djakarta. At the Djakarta airport, though, before I got into a taxi, Chaban told me he wanted to be there when I told Machmud about the Rahimat skirmish. I did not much care, and assented.

Within an hour of our landing at the airport, I had gotten in touch with Machmud and told him everything that had happened at the Sumatra cottage, but did not mention the falling-out with Chaban. I said I wanted to talk with him, though, and it was he who suggested he come to my small headquarters in the closed-down annex building.

Machmud came in the early evening, and he had Surabaya with him. Chaban and I were both there, waiting for them. After greetings and some small talk, Surabaya expressed his disappointment in losing Yussef Batak.

'I expected there might be casualties,' he said, sighing. 'But Batak was a particularly good man.'

'You're damned right he was,' I said. Batak had become a friend to me, in this brief time. I would never forget his bloody corpse there beside the cottage, his eyes staring unseeing into a hot yellow sky.

Chaban spoke up now. 'Rainey thinks I am responsible for Batak's death,' he said. He was leaning against a far wall, keeping apart from me. His manner, as usual, was arrogant and aloof.

Machmud and Surabaya both looked over at me. They were dressed in plain civilian suits, and Machmud was again wearing the sunglasses to hide his face from the world.

'What is this about, Rainey?' he asked.

I looked from Machmud to Chaban. 'He doesn't follow orders,' I said curtly. 'If he had kept down as I told him, he wouldn't have drawn fire down on Batak. He's an insubordinate bastard and I can't work with him.'

There was an embarrassed silence in the room. We were all standing, and the standing suddenly seemed uncomfortable. Machmud glanced at Chaban again, and cleared his throat. 'Do you have an answer to this, Chaban?'

Chaban was maddeningly cool. 'Rainey liked Batak, and does not like me. Batak was not a threat to his leadership, and I suspect that he thinks I am. He wants to think I am responsible for Batak's death, because that makes him feel better. I think Batak's death had nothing to do with my method of approaching the cottage. As to following Rainey's orders, I protest that every man must be allowed to make certain decisions on his own, when his life is on the line. I followed Rainey's orders as best I could.'

Anger welled up inside me. He made it all sound so damned innocent. I swallowed the emotion back. 'The hell you did,' I said. I turned to Machmud. 'Mr President, if you want me to finish this mission, I want somebody else to work with. Preferably another man from your military, like Batak. One should suffice.'

Machmud pursed his lips. I was putting him on the spot, but did not care. I had had it with Chaban.

Surabaya intervened and gave Machmud time to think. 'Rainey,' he began somberly, 'we are in the middle of something very important here. And we are succeeding, it would seem. But in spite of our success, lives are still at stake. Every day that passes exposes us all to further danger, until Quan and Afandi, and even Rublev, are removed from this death-struggle. Do you think we can afford to reorganize your tiny strike force, in the center of this vortex of violence?'

'Surely we could have another man available within hours,' I countered.

Machmud now turned to me. 'Batak was the best we could find for you, Rainey. It would be very difficult to come up with anyone with half his skills. This is not the American CIA we are talking about, after all. No, I'm afraid anybody I could quickly find for you would fall far short of replacing Chaban and his special skills.'

Chaban kept his silence. He did not have to say any more, and he knew it. I hated him for being such a clever bastard.

'Chaban's special skills have so far helped kill a couple of the enemy, and in the process killed Batak and damn near aborted the operation,' I said deliberately. 'How great an asset has his quick gun been, on balance?'

Machmud went and sat at the table near him, and drummed slim fingers on it. 'I am asking you as a special favor, Rainey. Do not ask me to dispense with Chaban's services at this time. Try to see this through with him. We are very close to victory.'

Chaban grunted. 'If he wants out of this, I will take the job on alone. I don't need anybody else. I will hand you Quan's and Afandi's heads within forty-eight hours.'

Machmud glanced toward Chaban, and I think he bought Chaban's boast. Surabaya came over to me. 'Please, Rainey,' he said.

Machmud turned to me again. 'If you will keep Chaban on, Rainey, I will renew my offer to give you a bonus of ten thousand American dollars. And you will have it immediately.'

I saw the scowl develop on Chaban's face when he heard that. I knew that he was already getting much less than me, and it bugged him to think that I would be paid even more just to keep him on. It was probably for that reason alone that I relented.

'All right, Mr President,' I said heavily. 'I'll give it another try with Chaban. But I won't like it.'

Chaban snorted, across the room. Surabaya turned to him darkly.

Machmud ignored Chaban, rising and offering me his hand. 'I appreciate this effort on your part, Rainey. I'm sure that you and Chaban will be able to work together through this final phase of our operation. You, of course, will still be in charge.' He glanced at Chaban, and then back at me. Chaban just scowled.

I nodded. 'We'll see how it goes,' I said.

Surabaya turned to Chaban. 'Do you accept Rainey's leadership, Chaban?'

Chaban shrugged eloquently. 'Have I ever rejected it?' he asked smoothly.

'Then please shake Rainey's hand on it,' Surabaya insisted to him.

Chaban gave him an acid look, then moved off the wall reluctantly and came over to me. He had, after all, won a small victory. 'I will shake it if he offers it,' he said.

I stuck my hand out stiffly. Chaban took it in a crunching grip, and I gripped back. We stood there for a long moment, each testing the other, then the grips lessened and contact was broken.

'Very nice,' Surabaya smiled.

But I knew better.

Machmud and Surabaya were pressing for me to go after Colonel Nur Afandi next. Quan was continuing to hole up, with the death of Rahimat following so close on the Malik and Solkar killings. Machmud was not even certain exactly where he was. But Colonel Afandi of the First Army, stationed not far from Djakarta, had gotten his back up about the killings, and I had word from an informant that he was out looking for Machmud's 'hired killers'. He supposedly had loyal subordinates out gathering information with the idea that there was a secret plot to kill off all leftist leaders who innocently opposed governmental policy. The colonel was allegedly out with these soldiers himself, asking questions of known informants and other sources. This meant that Afandi himself, of course, was more vulnerable physically at that time – and that was just what Machmud wanted.

The evidence indicated that Quan and Afandi were the big guns in the PLA coup plot, outside of Rublev the inciter. Quan was the one with the most popular following, but Afandi was a tough army man who got things done and had the guts and ability to kill, personally, if the need arose. He had risen through the ranks, like Malik in the labor organizations, and was considered a brilliant tactician by his superiors like Surabaya and Machmud. But it had also been clear that he was a potentially dangerous man, even before the hard evidence was gathered against him. Machmud had him figured as an overambitious fellow who had joined PLA and Quan for the very selfish motive of gaining quick power, regardless of the kind of politics he had to embrace to get it.

The same evening that Chaban and I had had our talk with Machmud and Surabaya, I went alone to a rendezvous with an informant that Surabaya had put me onto. The fellow's name was Wasfi, and I met him in the bar of the Hotel Indonesia. There was just a couple of other customers at the time, so we had no trouble with privacy. I took a seat across a small table from him, in a dark corner. He was a thin, small man who wore a dirty white turban.

'All right, Wasfi,' I said when my drink had come. 'What do you have?'

Wasfi was the type who kept shooting his glance around the room to make sure someone had not sneaked up on him to listen. He also had a nervous tic that pulled at the side of his face. It was all very distracting.

'The cost is a thousand rupiahs, *apa mengarti*?'

'Yes, yes,' I said. 'It will come directly from the general.'

He nodded his understanding. 'Okay, Joe.' His eyes flicked about, watching the room, and his cheek jerked visibly. He was in the wrong business. 'The colonel will be at the Officers' Club tomorrow night.'

'Oh?'

'He may not take personal guards inside,' Wasfi continued.

'Are you sure?'

He shrugged. 'Ask the general.'

I thought about that. 'What will he be doing there?'

'It is thought that he will be attempting to find out what Surabaya has been organizing against him.'

I took a deep breath. That made a lot of sense.

'There is a rumor that there will be more killings,' Wasfi went on. 'And soon.'

The rumor was probably true, too. I knew that Quan and Afandi had guessed by now that there was a concerted counter-plot against them, just as secret as theirs, and that their lives now depended on their success against Machmud and his government. Time was running out for us fast.

'Yes,' I said. 'Is that all?'

He thought. 'Ah. One more thing. Afandi was seen in the presence of a foreigner yesterday.'

'And what did this man look like?' I said.

'I do not know, *toean.* But his name was heard. It was something like Rub-off.'

'Rublev?' I said.

'That is probably it, *toean.*'

If any doubt still lingered about Rublev's involvement, it was now gone. Rublev was stepping in to give advice in the middle of PLA's new trouble.

'Okay,' I finally said. 'We'll be in touch, Wasfi.'

'Yes, *toean,*' he replied, the tic jerking his face.

A moment later he was gone. I sat there nursing my drink, thinking about Afandi and Rublev and Quan. They were a dangerous trio, even without their dead comrades. I would have to go carefully. But I had to agree with Machmud now. Colonel Afandi seemed to be our next target.

I swigged the last of my drink and got up and left the bar. Out in the spacious lobby, several tourists stood around, laughing and talking amiably. I found myself envying them just a little. Their lives were very uncomplicated at the moment. They were enjoying the fruits of their labors. I wondered sometimes if I would ever find myself in a hotel lobby with nothing on my mind but how to entertain myself.

I turned to head across the lobby to the door, and as I did so, I almost walked into another man who was going into the bar.

I recognized his square face with the slightly-almond-shaped eyes immediately, and the rather tall, athletic build. They belonged to Vasil Rublev.

Rublev stopped and stared at me openly for a long moment, in violation of every rule of his profession. He had obviously seen me before, or else had viewed some pretty good photographs, as I had of him. I knew in that instant that my cover was blown and that our deadly little war against each other would be much more out in the open from this moment on.

'You're Rainey,' he said quietly. His hard eyes narrowed just slightly on me. I saw the small bulge under his tight-fitting jacket and knew that it was a gun of some kind.

'I believe you have the advantage of me,' I lied.

'No, I don't,' he said to me sourly.

'All right, Rublev, you're right,' I said in a low voice. 'I recognized you, too.'

'So you are the Machmud recruit,' he said tautly.

'And you're the Mokri Dela bastard who started this whole bloody mess,' I said evenly.

His face darkened. He was a dangerous-looking man. His eyes were as hard as Chaban's, but there was much more intelligence in them. In that moment, I knew that Rublev and those who sent him were the real enemies of Machmud and Indonesia.

He spoke English flawlessly. 'I don't know what you're talking about,' he said angrily. 'I am a Russian consulate employee. I have friends in Djakarta who hope for eventual liberation of the people here from monarchistic leaders and their imperialistic partners in crime. But I know nothing of blood, Mr Rainey. That is your interest, however, I suspect.'

I raised my eyebrows. 'I'm not a violent man, Rublev. I'm here to discuss a private arms deal with officials here. I'm a businessman.'

His face darkened further. 'I know very well who you are, Rainey. You are a mercenary soldier playing at cloak-and-dagger. I suggest you abandon this game before it becomes too complex for you.'

My back was up now, too. I wished we were not in a crowded hotel lobby, just as Rublev must have wished it. If the confrontation had taken place in private, only one of us would have walked away from it.

'And I suggest,' I countered, 'that you watch over your shoulder, Rublev. The end-game seems to be coming up very quickly for you.'

I walked on past him then, leaving him fuming.

I did not immediately leave the hotel. I tried to find Wasfi, who had been going to eat before leaving. I wanted to put him onto Rublev, hoping he could follow him somewhere. But Wasfi had apparently left the building.

When I went out to the rented Fiat, on a side street beside the hotel, I was careful. Rublev would stick a big feather in his cap if he managed to kill me tonight, I thought. Just as I would figure most of it was over if I could get to him.

There was nobody on the dark street. I checked inside the car before I got in, and satisfied myself nobody was waiting in it for me. Next I went and raised the bonnet at the rear of the car, and the luggage-compartment lid at the front. I found no evidence that the car had been tampered with.

I got in and sat there for a moment, wondering just how much Rublev and the PLA people knew. They might have a considerably better network of informants than we had. Rublev would be an expert at developing that sort of system.

Finally I drove on back to the annex where Chaban and I were still staying. Chaban had gone out for the evening, too, to gather information on Ali Quan, and he was not back yet when I returned. I parked the car and went on upstairs and unlocked the door to the big room carefully.

We kept the lights on all the time, and they were off.

That meant little, though, because Chaban was so independent in his actions that he was always breaking little rules. I stepped into the room with the Star drawn nevertheless, being cautious. A dim light came into the room from the windows on one wall. But most of the room was in deep shadow. I moved quickly out of the doorway as I came in, and shut the door behind me.

There was no movement anywhere, and no sound. But I had the feeling that I was not alone in the room. I had been going to walk to the center of the room to pull the overhead light on – the nearest one to me – but realized now that that would make me a perfect target when the light came on.

I stood there against the wall, not breathing, listening and waiting. Somewhere outside a dog barked for a moment. I could hear a car go past on the street. After that, there was silence again.

I listened, holding my breath.

I scanned the dark room with my eyes.

I heard the indistinct sound of breathing.

There was no doubt now. There was someone else in the room with me.

My mind whirled. It could be the bastard Chaban, lying in ambush to make good on his threat to me. With me dead, Machmud would have to go with Chaban. Chaban could make it look as if there had been a struggle with an intruder.

But the more likely thing was, I knew, that Rublev had found out where our headquarters was located, and had beat me back here, and was now waiting to stick that feather into his cap.

I ducked low and found myself in deeper shadow. I moved along the wall so that my position would not be known. My potential assailant knew now that I was not going for the light. That meant that the attack might commence at any moment.

I moved again, and failed to see an empty liquor bottle. Chaban had apparently set on the floor there. I hit it with my foot, and it fell over, making a tinkling sound but not breaking. In the next split-second, I heard a sharp hissing sound from across the room. My eye caught the small flash of the silenced shot, and the wall chipped beside my head.

I swore and dived to the floor at the side of an old overstuffed chair. The kissing sound smacked the silence again as I rolled twice on the floor. One slug chewed up tile beside me and the second one thumped into the stuffing of the chair.

Coming up with the Star .45 in hand, I fired now toward the outline of a shadow I saw behind the flashes. The Star banged out loudly in the big room, but I missed my target, and then I saw the dark form hurtling across the room toward one of the closed windows.

I rolled again, came up in position, and steadied the Star on my elbows, lying prone. I fired again as the figure of Rublev streaked across the darkness, and I thought I had hit him but he kept going. In the dim light from the window I could see his square face indistinctly, and then he hurled himself against the window.

There was a loud crashing noise as he went through glass and sash and disappeared from my view. I heard a thump on a low roof outside and then a rolling sound. I scrambled to my feet and ran to the window and leaned out, knowing I was making myself an excellent target. But Rublev was gone, as if by magic. He had landed on the roof outside the window and then dropped to the ground from there, and was now on his way to a car somewhere.

I came out of the window and leaned heavily against the wall there. A slug had bounced off the floor and grazed my side and

I felt a wetness there now, and the beginning of a burning sensation.

It had been close. Rublev's ambush had failed, but not by much. Failure was not a usual thing with him, I was certain.

I had been very lucky.

Nine

Chaban and I moved out of the annex that night, as soon as he returned.

I figured that if Rublev came back, he would have hired PLA guns with him the next time. I had been fortunate that he had not had time to bring them on his first visit.

Chaban was for staying at the annex and waiting for Rublev to come back, and be prepared for him. 'Why should we run from them, Rainey?' He was very cocky about it all, not having seen Rublev's deadly efficiency.

But I explained to him as patiently as I could that that was much too risky for our operation. Rublev might not risk his own life the second time. And we would end up battling it out with hired flunkies. Beating them would mean nothing, and losing to them would mean that Machmud and his government was in immediate and serious trouble, despite the loss by PLA of three of its leaders.

We moved into a sleazy hotel on the south side of the city, far from the annex building. It was a run-down place with roaches in the corners and a faded photograph of President Suharto – one of Machmud's predecessors – hanging askew over one of the twin beds.

Chaban hated it and made no bones about it. I reminded him that he would not have to get used to it. All of this would be over in a few days, I was sure, one way or the other. He threatened to stay apart from me at a better place. I told him to go ahead, and I would handle the rest of the operation alone.

He stayed.

That first night was a long one. I could hear rats scurrying about the room all night. Chaban, despite all his complaining, slept like a log. When he rose the next morning, though, he was in a foul mood.

'*Mon Dieu*, Rainey!' he grumbled as he cleaned the Mauser carefully, still undressed on the edge of his bed. 'Let us get this silliness over with!'

'Have patience, Chaban,' I told him, sipping a cup of black coffee I had sent down for. 'Tonight we make our try for Afandi.'

'Tonight?' he said with new interest.

'Tonight. At the Officers' Club, only a few blocks from here. The colonel will be there for part of the evening. I have it from one of Surabaya's sources. It sounds right.'

'Right in what way?' Chaban said acidly.

'In a tactical way,' I replied, deciding not to explain it all to this bastard, who would have only criticism anyway. 'We'll take him after he gets inside, separated from his accompanying soldiers.'

'Inside?' he said. 'I make a point of never making a hit inside a public building or enclosure. There can be too many sudden heroes getting in the way when you try to leave.'

'There isn't any better way,' I said carefully. 'We go in, Chaban. I'm calling the shots, remember?'

He gave me a chilling look. I thought maybe he had mellowed, having to live with me in close quarters. But Chaban was a little crazy in his head, it seemed. 'I remember, Rainey,' he said darkly. 'I also recall clearly that we still have a score to settle. Don't think I will forget.'

I grunted. 'You're sick, Chaban. I recommend you take the money from this job and hire a good psychiatrist. There's no better way you could spend it.'

'Go to hell, Rainey,' he told me.

There was a knock on the door. I got up and went over to it, drawing the Star. 'Yes?'

The accented English came through the door. 'Mr Smith, there is a call for you.' It was the dark-skinned clerk from the lobby.

I opened up. 'Who is it?' I asked the short fellow.

'I do not know, Mr Smith.'

I turned to Chaban. 'Don't leave the room,' I said. I holstered the Star then and left, following the clerk down to the desk.

I was not surprised that it was Machmud on the other end, when I picked up the phone at the desk. When he began talking, I could hear the tension and fear in his voice, and what he was saying gave me quite a shock.

'It is Surabaya, Rainey,' he said in a tight, high voice. 'They got him.'

'What?'

'He was leaving his bachelor apartment this morning. Just an hour or so ago. They were outside waiting for him.'

'They killed him?' I said hollowly.

'I think so. My report is a sketchy one. I'm on my way over there now. The ambulance has not even arrived yet.'

'What the hell happened to the two men who were going around with him?' I said. In the past twenty-four hours, both Surabaya and Machmud had been doubling up on their personal bodyguard. Surabaya had used two top-notch Guard soldiers.

'They were dead when he came out of the building,' Machmud told me. 'It's quite terrible, Rainey! I'm alone now! We are losing the fight to these madmen!'

'Calm down, Mr President,' I said quietly.

There was a heavy silence on the other end. I looked around to make sure the clerk was giving me privacy. He had gone out to the rear of the building to do some chore there. I spoke again into the receiver.

'We haven't lost the fight,' I said urgently. 'You stay put. Don't leave your offices to go there or anywhere else. They may be expecting you to do something foolish now, and be waiting somewhere for you. Do you understand me, sir?'

Another short silence. 'Yes, Rainey.'

'Good,' I said. 'I'm on my way to Surabaya's place. I'll give you a report just as soon as I can.'

I hung up and just stood there for a moment. The opposition meant business, all right. They had not been scared out by our counter-measures. If anything, they were accelerating their own offensive.

The clerk came into the small lobby carrying a case of beer. He stopped and stared at me. 'Is something wrong, Mr Smith?'

'No, no,' I said absently. 'Just tell Mr Brown upstairs that

I'm leaving for a short while, but will be back by mid-morning. Okay?'

'Sure, okay.'

I grabbed a cab just outside the door then, and gave the fellow a big tip to hurry, and he drove me to Surabaya's like a maniac. When I got there, there were policemen outside the rather modern building, and an ambulance had arrived. I walked over to the stretcher and bent over Surabaya, and saw that his eyes were open. At least he was not dead.

'General, it's Rainey,' I said quietly.

'Hey, you!' a policeman said in Indonesian. 'Get away from there!'

Surabaya waved the fellow away feebly, gesturing that I was all right. He looked up at me. There was a sheet over him, and an attendant was tying his feet to the stretcher in preparation to leaving with him. 'Hello, Rainey,' he said weakly.

I pulled the sheet down gently and saw the three bloody places on him. One was just a flesh wound in the side, but the others were central – one in the low chest and the other in the abdomen. Surabaya had a fighting chance, but he was not in good shape.

'They really got to you, didn't they, General?' I said.

Surabaya licked his lips. 'My bodyguards that you insisted I keep with me were waiting – out here at the car. They had been shot, over and over. Apparently with – silenced guns.'

I looked at the other two stretchers, with the white coverings up over the heads of the guards. Blood was already soaking through the covers. One stretcher was being loaded into a second ambulance that had just driven up. Two attendants were now ready to take Surabaya. I hurried my few questions.

'Did you see anybody?' I asked.

'Yes. There were two gunmen out here on foot. I had never – seen either of them before. They are obviously two of those hired – at Palembang. But there was a third man – who fired from a waiting car. I got a look at him, Rainey. It was Rublev.'

'Sonofabitch,' I muttered. 'That bastard is busy. He tried to kill me last night.'

'Get that damnable – Russian,' he gritted out.

I nodded to the attendants, and they picked the stretcher up.

'Okay, General,' I said. 'But you stick with this and beat it, you hear me?'

'All right, Rainey,' he said.

They carried him to the waiting ambulance then, and a moment later drove away with him. I wondered if he would make it. If not, a strong ally of Machmud was gone, and my battle was partly lost, no matter whether I killed the rest of the plotters or not.

The same policeman came up to me again, an officious man in a dark uniform. 'All right, mister. You must leave now. An investigation is going on here.' He spoke in Indonesian, and I could not follow it well.

I turned to him grimly. 'Listen,' I said, 'do you understand English?'

He shrugged. 'A little.'

'Then listen to what I have to say. I am a friend of the general, and I too am making an investigation here – '

'That is not possible,' he said, interrupting me with an emphatic shake of his head. 'Only police are here now, sir. I have my orders, and – '

I jerked an I.D. out of my pocket, one given me by Machmud himself for just such an emergency. It gave my rank in the Presidential Guard, and was a special pass to all governmental agencies and functions.

'Do you see the President's signature there?' I said.

His face changed. 'Yes.'

'I am making an investigation of these assassination attempts. I am not to be impeded in the conduct of my business. Would you like to call the President and check me out?'

He grinned tightly. 'That will not be necessary, sir. If you need any help, please ask us.'

'I'll keep that in mind,' I said.

He strolled away, and I walked over to a subordinate officer. 'Are there any witnesses besides the general?' I asked in Indonesian.

'I believe not, sir,' he told me.

I turned and stared along the hibiscus-lined walk to the street, wishing someone had been there to get a license number or a description of one of the gunmen accompanying Rublev.

Anything might help, in the long run. But the long run was not very long, in this case, I suspected.

I thought of calling the Russian embassy, consular section, posing as someone official and asking Rublev's local address. But then Surabaya was certain that even the consul people might think Rublev had left town. Mokri Dela was a very secretive outfit. And if Rublev had given the consul an address, he would not be so dumb as to be there still, since our open confrontation.

I looked around the area, trying to avoid the eyes of the policemen. I don't know what I hoped to find, but I figured it did not hurt to look. I was about ready to leave when I spotted the small object under a shrub, near the walk.

I went over and picked it up. No policeman had seen me, and that was good. I did not want a fight over who kept this bit of evidence.

I turned it over in my hand. It was a matchbook with all the matches gone. It advertised a café in Palembang. That would suggest it was owned by one of the gunmen, all right. But it would avail me nothing to go looking in a Palembang café at this stage of the game. The matchbook itself was ancient history. I thought of fingerprints, and realized it would be impossible to get them off that soft cardboard. Also, I did not have the time for a formal police-bureau type investigation. There were killers on the streets waving guns around.

I examined the item more carefully and saw the smudge of oil on its back side. I put it to my nose, and a familiar odor came to me. The oil was a particular kind. While I was still trying to recall exactly which one, I saw the tiny particle of bright metal clinging to the paper.

I looked at it carefully, then picked it off and rolled it in my fingers. It was a small shaving from a metal lathe. And the oil was machine-shop oil, I realized now.

I stuffed the matchbook into my pocket and turned and walked to the taxi that was still waiting for me down the street. No policeman accosted me as I left. I was a friend of the President.

I stopped at a bar I knew on the way back to the hotel, called the hospital and found out that Surabaya's chances of survival were good. That pleased me. I called Machmud and relayed the information to him, and he was very emotional about it. When I got off the phone to him, I took the taxi on back to the hotel. Chaban was not there. He had left a note for me, saying he was going out for ten minutes for something to eat. He had taken the Fiat.

Angry, I went down to the clerk and found out that Chaban had already been gone almost a half hour. He had disobeyed another direct order, and had fouled up my plan to take him with me on my run-down of the machine shop.

I looked through the telephone directory at the hotel, and found there were only three machine shops listed in Djakarta. There may have been others without phones, but I could not concern myself with that possibility. One of those listed was on the same side of town as the Russian embassy, Surabaya's apartment, and a munitions dump that was under the jurisdiction of Afandi's First Army. I made a call there and found out that the number had been disconnected. Which probably meant it was closed down. Another call – to another shop – revealed the clincher. Ali Quan owned the closed-down place.

When I got outside on the street, Chaban was nowhere in sight, but my taxi was still there, waiting for another fare. I got in again, and gave the driver the address of the machine shop.

We were there in fifteen minutes. I asked the driver to let me off a block away, and then dismissed him. A few minutes later I arrived at the place.

It was in an industrial neighborhood, if it could be called that in Djakarta. The street was unpaved and dusty, and there were a lot of old warehouse-type buildings, some closed down. There were also some empty lots, weed-grown. Down the street, some workers moved about in the yard of a boat-building business.

The machine shop was in a small, corrugated-iron building that was off the street about twenty yards. The windows were all boarded up, and the front door was locked with a heavy padlock. There was no evidence of anyone being about. I walked around to the rear, and found a fenced-in area with an unlocked gate. I went in, and walked between piles of metal shavings and scrap metal. There was a rusty metal and wood door at the building, and it was closed, but unlocked.

I drew the Star and opened the door. Through the opening I could see several metal lathes up near the front of a big room that apparently took up the entire building. The smell of machine oil – a magnification of the whiff I had gotten from the matchbook – assailed my nostrils. I stepped through the doorway, and a shot rang out.

The first shot missed me by inches, but the second one grazed my upper left arm. I yelled and dived for the concrete floor, hitting there in a pile of metal shavings. A third shot chipped up concrete beside my head and sprayed its dust into my face.

I turned and saw the big revolver aimed at my face. A hard, tough-looking oriental stood behind it. His finger whitened over the trigger.

I fired the Star first, hitting the oriental in the belly.

Apparently he had not seen the Star, and his eyes popped wide in surprise as he went stumbling over a wooden bench and dragged it to the floor with him with a crashing sound.

He still had the gun. He held his bloody mid-section with his left hand and raised the revolver – a Webley .38 – to try to finish me off with the big-nosed handgun.

I had fallen beside a stack of metal crates, or boxes. I shoved at them with my foot now, and they toppled toward the broad-faced thug on the floor – one of Surabaya's assailants, I was certain. He looked from me to them, and yelled something unintelligible as they came crashing down on him, some of them heavy with machine parts.

They hit him across his body and head, and clattered on the concrete beside him. I heard another muffled yell as they crunched him under their weight, bounced off him and rolled over on the floor.

When it was over, he had lost the gun, and lay under two of the boxes, one on his chest. He was wheezing heavily, and I figured one of them had busted his ribs. Another had mashed the right side of his face, and it was bloody and bluish, his right eye closing very rapidly.

I got up onto my knee, holding my gunshot arm. It was a shallow wound, but painful as hell. I went and knelt over him, and saw that he was a lot worse off than me.

'Okay, you sonofabitch,' I growled. 'Where is Quan holed up? Where is that damned Rublev? He was with you this morning.'

He shook his head. 'I don't know,' he replied in thickly accented English.

I holstered the Star and picked up an iron bar that lay on the floor near me. It was about two feet in length. I let it touch his face gently. He winced, breathing hard. There was fear now in the slitted eyes.

'You want me to mash you up good?' I asked him seriously.

He eyed the bar sidewise. 'I do not – see Quan – for days.'

'You tried to kill General Surabaya this morning, you bastard,' I told him. 'You were with Rublev. Surabaya told me.'

He was surprised to hear that Surabaya was still alive.

'Now you tell me where I can find Rublev. The coup is over for you, anyway. Tell me now, or I'll work you over carefully with this. You understand?' I moved the bar on the bloody and bruised side of his face, and he hissed in pain.

'He left me and – Hara here not long ago. He did not say – where he was going.'

'Hara is the other man who was with you at Surabaya's place?'

He nodded.

'Where does Rublev stay at night?' I pursued.

'I don't know. We call him at a number.'

'What number?'

He recited it to me, and I memorized it. I knelt there and thought over what he had said. I figured he had told me everything he knew that was important to me. I tightened my grip on the iron bar, and he saw the slight movement.

'I told you – everything!' he grated out.

I had executed spies in Africa and Lebanon, in my little wars in those places. I could execute an executioner now. I knew it was impractical to turn him over to the police, and he was too dangerous to turn loose. It was that simple.

I brought the bar down across his face in one savage strike. It caught him diagonally across his head, fracturing his nose and cheek and caving his face and forehead in.

His whole body stiffened in shock, his hands grabbing at the air. His bladder emptied into his trousers, his foot punched at the floor violently, and then he was lifeless.

I stared at the bloody bar for a moment, and at the gunman's featureless face, and then threw the bar to the floor. I rose and looked around me. There seemed to be no other evidence that would help me find Rublev or Quan. I headed for the rear door again.

I still had a few very dangerous days ahead of me. If I kept moving, I might be tougher to kill, in the end of this ugly game that Rublev played so well.

I just might avoid a sudden-death finish.

It was nice to think so, anyway.

Ten

My arm was bandaged up at the hospital when I stopped to see how Surabaya was doing. He had been out of surgery for an hour, all the lead had been pulled out of him, and no vital organs had been hit. He was going to recover.

I directed the police there to triple the guard on him. They checked with Machmud before they would do it, and then they followed orders. By the time I left the hospital, Surabaya's floor looked like a military encampment.

That was the way I wanted it.

Machmud helped me get the address for the phone number the gunman had divulged to me. It was an apartment in an old tenement building only a few blocks from the machine shop. I decided to check it out immediately.

Stopping at the hotel again for Chaban, I finally found him there at about noon. He was nursing a bottle of bourbon. I slammed the room door behind me in anger.

'Goddam it, Chaban,' I said.

He was propped against a wall, on his cot. He eyed me with disdain. 'What's the matter, Rainey? Are you going to make an issue of my going out for something to eat?'

'I needed the Fiat, damn it. I told you to stay put.'

'I was out only a few minutes,' he argued.

'Bullshit,' I told him.

He shrugged. I walked over to him, grabbed the bottle away from him, and hurled it across the room. It crashed against the wall over there, and the contents spattered everywhere. Chaban rose with a scowl, ready to hit me. I turned back to him with the Star in hand, sticking the muzzle up to his face.

'Go ahead, damn you,' I said. 'Tempt me.'

Chaban stared at the gun muzzle, then he began laughing. I fought to control my anger.

'Would you really kill me in cold blood, Rainey? I thought you were not the type.'

I swallowed the anger back. 'Get your jacket on,' I said. 'We're going after Rublev.'

His eyes narrowed down on my face. I dropped the gun to my side. 'Now,' I said.

'You know where Rublev is hiding out?'

'No thanks to you,' I said. 'I have an address. I don't know whether he'll be there or not. But I'm going to check it out.' I holstered the Star. 'Let's go.'

Chaban did not need another invitation. He had been chafing for action. We took the Fiat to the address I had been given, and arrived there in the early afternoon.

The neighborhood was one of the oldest ones in Djakarta, and was now mostly commercial. The address given for Rublev was in a falling-down building with half the flats closed up. He knew how to pick them. I had stayed in such places myself when trying to keep out of sight.

We parked the Fiat in an empty lot down the street and hoped nobody noticed. Chaban suggested approaching by the rear entrance of the building, and I thought the idea was a good one. There was an alleyway littered with garbage and trash, and a metal door that stood half open. He went through it and into a corridor. There was a wooden stairway to an upper floor, where Rublev's room was supposedly located.

We climbed the stairs very carefully, Chaban in front. There was no sign of life in the building. Old newspapers and other litter decorated the stairs. There was an ugly odor to the place that I could not quite identify. We came out on a second-floor corridor that was feebly lighted, with scarred walls and a crumbling plaster ceiling. Rublev's room was halfway down, with the number 204 on its door.

Chaban listened at the door and heard nothing. He tried the door and it was locked.

I stepped in and used a lock-pick carefully. There was a dull click when the tumbler fell. I turned the knob and pushed the door open slightly. I could see nothing. Chaban made a gesture that he would go on in, and I assented. He stepped back slightly and kicked at the open door and it banged inward.

Chaban stormed into the room with the Mauser drawn, and I went in right after him. There was nobody there. There was a private bath off a corner of the room, with its small door open, and Chaban checked it out and came up empty.

We holstered our guns.

Chaban muttered a couple of obscenities. '*Attendez ici,*' he added then, telling me to wait in the room. 'I will see if there is a *concierge.*'

'Don't bother,' I told him. 'Rublev has moved out on us.'

Chaban seemed nettled by my conclusion. 'How can you be sure of that?'

I looked around the room. There was a bed, unmade, and a table and a couple of chairs. On the bed and table were a few personal effects: a shirt, an American magazine, half a package of Turkish cigarettes. But nothing really important to Rublev was there.

I went to a wardrobe on the wall and opened it. There was nothing in it except a discarded newspaper. 'Nothing necessary to daily living has been left here,' I said.

'Then why did he leave anything?' Chaban said wryly.

I shrugged. 'To keep us guessing.'

Chaban began looking through the room. He pulled the mattress off the bed before I could stop him, and then headed for a night table. He was about to open the drawer, when I yelled at him.

'Hold it, Chaban!' I called out.

He turned to me darkly, then reached for the drawer again. I stepped over and quickly caught his hand in my firm grip.

'What's the matter with you, Rainey?' he yelled.

Our eyes met at close quarters, and his were filled with sudden resentment. 'Look at the bottom edge of the drawer,' I said to him quietly, still holding his hand.

He glanced at the table, then pulled his hand free and knelt down to look at the drawer. I squatted beside him and pointed to the small wire running along the under surface.

'It's booby-trapped,' I said heavily. 'That's why Rublev left some of his things, to make us think he was still using the room.

That way, we would feel free to search it casually.'

Chaban rose, and I did, too. 'You damn near blew us both up, Chaban,' I said seriously. 'If you had ever had a man stalk you, instead of always being the hunter yourself, you would go more carefully.'

A normal man would have felt chagrin, or maybe even gratitude that I had saved his life. But not Chaban. I could see the new and increased resentment in his face. 'It was your idea to come and sneak around an apartment building today, Rainey. If I were in charge of this operation, I would be out killing Quan and Afandi, and to hell with the Russian. He is not worth the trouble.'

Before I could reply, Chaban turned and stalked back to the door. 'When you are finished with your game-playing here, I will be outside.'

A moment later, I was left in the room alone, trying to keep the rage inside me. I turned and double-checked the booby trap, and found that the explosives were inside the drawer itself, ready to go up in our faces.

It had been a devilishly clever move by Rublev, and a very callous one. If a maintenance man had come into the room before we had gotten there, there would probably have been an innocent death.

I took a few minutes to disconnect the explosives, and then opened the drawer. There it was, in the middle of the drawer: enough plastic to blow the room apart.

I grew an even bigger respect for Rublev than I had had previously. He was a formidable opponent. His chances of winning this little chess game were excellent.

I searched the rest of the room then, but found nothing that would help locate Rublev.

I was at a dead end momentarily.

But all that might change that evening, at the Officers' Club.

It was not easy getting along with Chaban until evening came. I accomplished it by keeping away from him most of that time. Any time we spoke, Chaban was arrogant and offensive. It was almost as if he resented my saving him from the explosives.

At 9.15 I got a call from a paid informant whom I had

stationed outside the Officers' Club, on the parking lot. Colonel Nur Afandi had just entered the building in the company of two other men. My informant had not gotten a description of the men, except that they were in uniform.

I arrived at the parking lot of the Officers' Club just after 9.30 with Chaban. I had given strict instructions to my informant to leave the place immediately after reporting to me, so did not know for sure that Afandi was still there. But if he was there to try to learn about the counter-plot, as I had been told, he would probably be there a while.

Chaban snapped a three-inch silencer onto his Mauser automatic, and I screwed a four-inch one onto the Star, reducing its stubby look. The work we had to do inside the club was the kind that could attract a lot of attention, without the silencers. We got out of the car, and Chaban turned to me. His eyes were as hard as diamonds.

'After tonight, Rainey, we will be near the end. Do not think that this afternoon changed anything between us. When this is over, it will be you or me.'

'Up yours, Frenchman,' I told him.

He grunted an obscenity in his throat, and turned and headed for the rear door of the building. There were cars parked heavily in the lot between us and the door, and I watched them closely, and saw nothing to alert me to danger.

We were walking across the same lot where Surabaya and Asaban and I had been attacked by PLA gunmen when all this started, and Asaban had been violently killed. That memory came burning through to me like acid, and I got a bad feeling about the place that was irrational but very real.

We came to the door and Chaban preceded me into the building. We were both wearing military uniforms supplied by Machmud, and had fake I.D. We did not want any arguments about getting into the Officers' Club. We walked down a short entrance foyer and turned a corner into a waiting room, and found two men confronting us there, also in uniform, waiting outside a closed door of the club proper.

Chaban was only mildly surprised, but I was stunned. One man was Vasil Rublev, and the other was the PLA gunman I had seen a photo of when I first arrived in Djakarta and was being briefed by Surabaya.

'Kill them!' I said loudly to Chaban.

Rublev had also recognized me, and his eyes narrowed to slits. I went for the Star on my hip, in a break-open belt holster, and the gunman hurled himself at me. I did not get the Star free before his weight hit me hard, and we went down together.

As we hit, I heard Chaban mutter Rublev's name sourly as he went for the Mauser.

Rublev, too, hurled himself toward us, hitting Chaban before he could find the Mauser. He kicked into Chaban's groin. Chaban moved slightly and Rublev missed his target, the foot thumping into Chaban's right thigh. Rublev threw a backhand savagely into Chaban's face and head, though, and connected just as Chaban got his gun free. He grunted hard and fell against the wall near him, and slid to the floor, dazed and surprised by the ferocity of his opponent. I figured he was learning fast about the deadliness of Rublev.

But I was having my own troubles. The gunman had thrown two punches into my head, and now he was going for his own gun as we rolled on the floor. He was a broad-faced Indonesian with muscles on his muscles, and I was having a hell of a time with him. He got his revolver clear and I managed to grab that hand before he could turn the muzzle into my chest or face.

I got a glimpse of Rublev and Chaban as we rolled on the floor. Rublev had now drawn a Russian-made revolver – it looked like a 7.62 mm Nagant – and had Chaban beat. Chaban was just raising the Mauser to fire from the hip when the Nagant went off loudly in the corridor.

Chaban was hit in the chest, low. He jumped on the floor, his hard eyes going slightly wide as he realized what had happened to him. The Mauser went off and missed Rublev, the slug banging into the ceiling of the corridor behind Rublev.

Now the gunman had the revolver turned partially to me. I grabbed the gun with both hands and twisted hard, sweat popping out on me as it turned slowly. When it was aimed at the gunman's side, I made his finger squeeze the trigger, jamming the gun into his ribs at the same time. There was a muffled explosion and the gunman jerked away from me, then fell onto his side.

Chaban was out of it now, dying on the floor. Rublev turned the Nagant on me now, seeking me wildly with his hard eyes. I saw the muzzle find me, and his finger tighten over the trigger. I pulled the gunman over between me and Rublev just as Rublev fired.

The revolver roared again in the corridor, and the slug thumped into the gunman's side just beside my hand that held him as cover. I went for the Star again, still ducked behind the lifeless gunman.

Rublev swore in Russian and turned and ran for the outside door. I had the Star out now, and aimed carefully after him. He turned the corner we had just rounded, and I fired. The slug caromed off the plaster wall, narrowly missing Rublev's head.

Then Rublev was gone.

It was my turn to swear now. I pushed the dead body of the gunman off me awkwardly, and finally managed to get out from under. I rose groggily and went over and stood over Chaban. His eyes were still open, and he was alive. He looked up at me, his Mauser still in hand. His lips moved.

'Damn you, Rainey,' he said in his thick accent. 'You have – all the luck.'

He raised the Mauser and aimed it at my chest. I was too weak at the moment to move quickly. I looked down the big muzzle for a long moment, waiting for death. Then Chaban's eyes glazed over, and he slumped lifeless on the corridor floor.

The door to the club banged open, and two young army officers were there.

'What happened here?' the tallest one said loudly in Indonesian.

'We found these men here, waiting for Colonel Afandi,' I said quickly. 'I think they intended to kill him.'

I hoped that neither of them knew the gunman had come with Afandi.

'Good heavens!' the shorter one muttered.

'You go get an ambulance,' I said to the tall one. The insignia on my uniform outranked him. 'You take me to Colonel Afandi inside. I want to warn him. But do not make a commotion, please.'

They both nodded. The short one took me inside, and the tall one went to a phone as we walked through a dining room and into a game room where several officers were playing billiards. We went through that and to a study down a corridor. Afandi had been talking with an officer in there and now was coming toward the doorway just as we entered.

'Did I hear shooting?' Afandi said. He was a squarely-built, tough-looking man in his thirties, with medals on his tailored uniform. Behind him stood a slim, ugly-faced officer he had been talking with privately.

Afandi did not recognize me. I turned to the short fellow who had led me there. 'You may see to the fellow in the corridor,' I said.

He nodded and left. I closed the study door. When I turned back to Afandi, his eyes had narrowed on me. 'I asked you a question, Captain. What is going on outside?'

I drew the Star from its holster at my side, and Afandi looked at it curiously. Then he saw the silencer attached to its muzzle. His face changed very quickly.

'*You are the one!*' he hissed in a low breath.

'Good guess,' I said.

The young officer Afandi had been talking to found understanding in that moment, and went for the service revolver on his hip. He was an M.P. of some kind and wore the gun openly, like me. I saw the movement. At the same moment, Afandi got an ugly look on his face, and a growl began in his throat. Very bravely, I thought, he grabbed a chair beside him, a straight, spindly one, to hurl it at me.

I ignored Afandi, steadied the Star with both hands, and aimed past Afandi to the officer who now had his gun out and was aiming it at my chest. I fired at him twice, the Star cracked dully behind the silencer, and the slim fellow went dancing across the room like an Indonesian performer at the Nirwana Nightclub, hit in the middle and high chest. He smashed across a low table where drinks were sitting, and took it all down with him in a loud clatter. In that same instant, Afandi hurled the chair at me.

I ducked, but was hit across the arm and chest by the chair. Losing my balance, I went down hard. I held onto the Star .45. When I looked up, Afandi was standing over me with a heavy glass ashtray. He was going to smash my head like a melon with it.

'Die, damn you!' he grated out. He had the big glass object above his head, ready to hurl it down onto my face.

Before he could, though, I remembered the Star in my right hand, and fired from the hip. The cracking sound came again, and the slug hit Afandi under the left arm and ripped through his insides. He staggered backwards, shock in his broad face, the ashtray still above his head. Slowly the ashtray came down to chest level, and he clutched at it tightly there, his jaw working. He fell to his knees, staring past me.

I got up, feeling new bruises on my left arm and my chest. I kept the Star aimed at Afandi's face now.

'You chose a dangerous way to grab power, you bastard,' I said to him quietly.

He looked at me, and toppled onto his side. The big ashtray clattered across the floor. He lay there trying to breathe properly, and not making it. I bent over him.

'Where's Quan?' I said urgently. 'It's pretty much over now. You might as well spill your guts.'

He said nothing.

'Tell me where I can find Quan,' I said, 'and I'll get you a doctor.' But I knew he was dead.

He turned his head just slightly, gave me a dark, hate-filled look, and died there. His eyes still stared openly at me, as if cursing me beyond the grave.

I rose and stared down at him. One more down. But they had gotten Chaban now, too, and I was alone.

I turned to the door, and listened. Nobody had heard the commotion we made. I opened the door, the Star still in hand, and looked down the corridor. There was plenty of excitement out in the rear of the building yet, and that was keeping them too busy to notice what had happened up front.

I went into the foyer leading to the front entrance, and found myself alone. Closing the door to the study, I holstered the Star and walked calmly to the front doors and opened one and walked out of the building. Nobody stopped me. Nobody noticed.

I abandoned the Fiat at the rear and took a taxi back to the sleazy hotel alone. Chaban was no longer around to anger or threaten me. But somehow, I took little comfort in that situation.

I still had Quan and Rublev.

It was them, now – or me.

Eleven

The Officers' Club was closed down that evening, pending an investigation of the violence that occurred there.

The following morning, the newspaper headlines screamed about Afandi's death, and the 'blood bath' at the Officers' Club. The news was on all the radio stations and on the lips of every local who had access to the news media, and many who did not. There was a fairly good description of me in the paper, and the police were combing the city for me.

I was a hunted man.

Machmud could, of course, have let the truth about me trickle down through the high command at police headquarters. But he was concerned that, if he did, my value to him might be at an end. He was right, of course. But in the meantime, I had to be careful that I was not shot to death on the street by some over zealous cop.

The PLA, which was underground in Djakarta, reportedly were shocked by the wanton killing, they thought, of their leaders. PLA had a secret headquarters in Djakarta, a kind of meeting hall, which was known to police but which was not watched closely. The police thought of PLA as troublesome but not dangerous, and had no knowledge of the involvement of PLA leaders in the murderous plot against the government. Neither did the ordinary membership of PLA, who were mere dupes of Quan and the other leaders. Machmud had not shared his information against the leaders with the police, and Quan had not shared his grand plan with the membership, in case they would not assent to such a radical and conscienceless move.

I slept badly that night after the bloody confrontation at the Officers' Club. I was concerned about being alone for the grand finale, and I kept thinking Rublev might somehow have followed me to the hotel and be waiting to kill me in my sleep. But when morning finally came, I was still surprisingly alive, although very sleepy and tired.

I got a call from Machmud just a short time after I rose, while I was still reading the morning paper, with its bold-type headlines about the killings. Machmud was more upset about the loss of Chaban than I was, and hardly mentioned my successful killing of Afandi. All he could talk about was the fact that I now had to go against Quan and Rublev alone, if we did not hire more help. I said I did not want any more underlings.

'But, Rainey!' he argued. 'You said yourself that this is not a job for one man alone!'

'That was when there were half a dozen to worry over,' I told him. 'It's different, now.'

I could hear him sigh heavily, over the phone. I could see his slim professor's face in my mind. I wondered whether he was wearing the wire spectacles that he used when working in his office, or the prescription sunglasses that he had taken to hiding behind recently everywhere he went. 'Rainey, you are in charge, as I told you. But it is my life at stake, too. I can have two more assistants at your hotel room within an hour or so. You may need them. Quan knows now that he's fighting for his life.'

I shook his head vehemently, even though Machmud could not see me. I had had enough of assistants. Chaban had done it for me. 'If you insist on sending Santa's Helpers, Mr President,' I said firmly, 'I'll call it quits. You'll get your payment back, but I'll take off on the next plane to Hong Kong and let *you* figure out how to handle Quan.'

There was a heavy silence. Machmud did not like being spoken to in that manner. But I did not care. I was going to play the game out my way or not at all.

'You leave me little choice, Rainey,' he finally said. 'All right. Do it your way. Go it alone. But try to be careful, for God's sake. If I lose you, it will be too late for me to organize again against them.'

'I'm aware of that,' I said. He was thinking of Number One, right up to the last. But then, I never expected more than that from any political leader. 'But I promise not to be suicidal with my life, Mr President. At least I'll have only myself to depend on. That's best, I think, from here on out. How is Surabaya doing?'

'The general is considerably better,' said Machmud. 'He will be in the hospital for a while, of course. I spoke to him this morning just before calling you. He was pleased about Afandi. He was hopeful that this would all be over now in the next few days.'

I made a sound in my throat. I was weary. 'It had better be,' I said.

The squat, bulky and smooth-talking Ali Quan had disappeared off the face of the earth, it seemed. No one had seen or heard from him since the death of Rahimat. He had understood well by that time that there was an organized counter-plot and that his life was just as much in jeopardy as those he had put there on his own death list. Informants had checked with his home and at his offices, and the word was that he had left town on a business trip. But he had told no one where he was heading – or they were not talking.

One man who undoubtedly knew Quan's whereabouts was Vasil Rublev. But that Russian was even more slippery than Quan. Quan was the type who might run when the going got tough, I knew, and might now be in Hong Kong or Manila or Honolulu. Or he might be hiding out in the city at Rublev's insistence, feeding Rublev information that would help track me down and end my life. That was more likely. Because even though Quan might be planning to run, he could not just leave Djakarta at any time he felt like it, and in any way. I had two informants stationed at the airport and the train terminal, and he had no way of knowing Machmud did not have the roads blocked by the police. If Quan was planning to leave he would have to give it some thought and go about it carefully. So I figured he was probably still around. He had not had time to get out of Djakarta.

Machmud could not give me any good leads. There was a social club Quan belonged to, but which denied having seen Quan in over a week. I figured he could be holed up in a place like that, paying an employee for secrecy. Or Rublev could have found him a hotel room not unlike my own sleazy one, and told him to stay put until this was all over between Rublev and me. Quan was so well-known in the city, though, that he could not keep under cover anywhere for long without being spotted. Of course, he did not have to hide for long, with Rublev and me after each other like hungry sharks.

At mid-morning I felt a little better, and thought of Nellie Ullah. She was a girl who seemed to have her ear to the ground most of the time. She was currently employed only part-time, at an export house, but she still knew a lot of people in government circles from her days as a ministry secretary.

I had told her I did not want to see her again until this was all over, but now I wondered if she might have something of importance to me in the way of information. I called her at 10.15 and got no answer. I gave up on the idea of reaching her, and went out to find Sarasin, the informant. I was unsuccessful in finding him, too, and found myself going right by Nellie's flat at about noon. I stopped the taxi driver and paid him and went up to Nellie's place.

When I knocked on the door, I heard Nellie yell to come in. I stepped into the apartment, and heard water running in a shower. A moment later Nellie came out into the living room, naked as the day she was born. She held a towel in her right hand, but there was no attempt to cover herself.

She looked stupendous.

'Oh, my gosh! Jim! I thought it was a girl friend.'

'How lucky for me,' I grinned.

She dropped the towel with a smile, and came over to me, dripping wet. Her breasts moved beautifully, and her long dark hair clung wetly to her face. She came and pressed herself against me, making my light-colored suit dark with dampness.

'And for me, too, lover.'

She offered me her lips, and I could not resist. They were warm and wet and tasted fine. I found my hands suddenly slippery on her backside. I pushed her firmly away from me.

Her lovely eyebrows went up. 'What is the matter, love? My friend will not be here for a half hour, probably. We have time.'

I shook my head. 'I don't, Nellie. I'm here on business.'

'Oh, damn,' she said, sulking. A drop of water ran down from her hair and over one breast and hung there for a moment. I tried not to look.

'I was wondering if you could help me locate Ali Quan,' I told her.

A knowing look came on her face. 'You were at the Officers' Club last evening, weren't you?'

'Maybe,' I said.

'I worry about you, lover.'

I sighed. 'Quan has dropped out of sight. Have you heard anything about him?'

She furrowed her lovely brow, and put a hand on her bare hip, and her breasts jiggled. 'It's coincidental that you should ask. An assemblyman's secretary told my friend who will be here soon that she saw Quan just the other day. Day before yesterday, I believe.'

'Where?'

'Just on the street. In the 800 block of Djuanda, if I recall correctly.'

'Just walking?'

'I guess so. She did not mention that he was coming out of or going into any particular store or shop.'

'Anything else?' I asked.

'He was with a couple of tough-looking men,' said Nellie. 'I thought of you when I heard this, Jim, but I had no way of contacting you. Maybe you should give me a number where I can reach you?'

I took her chin in my hand. I wanted to take much more than that. 'Maybe I should steal your towel, just for asking,' I grinned, I picked it up off the floor, and rubbed at her shoulders, and over her breasts. The curves of her were full under my touch. I had to quit before it was too late. I had business to finish first. I laid the towel over her shoulder.

'That was nice, lover. Are you sure you don't have time? Just a little?' Her voice was low and sexy.

'I will soon,' I said. I forced myself to turn and walk to the door. I opened it, and looked over my shoulder. 'Don't tell your friend I asked.'

'No,' she said. 'Come back, Jim.' Her face was somber, and I knew what she meant.

'I promise,' I told her.

Out on the street again, I realized I had not gotten much from Nellie. The fact that Quan was seen on the street with his bodyguards meant little to me. Except to confirm my suspicion that Quan was probably still in the city, under Rublev's orders.

I went to a car hire agency and got myself another Fiat – the other one was abandoned at the Officers' Club – and by noon I was driving along the street named Djuanda, wondering why Quan was walking there a couple of days ago. I came to the 800 block and slowed down, looking at all the businesses along there. There were many tourist shops and cafes. Quan might have been merely having lunch or a drink. I swept the façades with my eyes, and spotted the travel agency.

A light went on inside my head. What if Quan had decided our side was winning, and was getting ready to abandon ship, after all, maybe without Rublev's help? It might be not only more convenient to pick up his plane tickets or whatever at a small, out-of-the-way agency, rather than going directly to the airline involved, but even safer, if he happened to know a clerk there who would keep it all quiet.

It was a far-out hunch, but I had little to lose by checking it out. I parked the Fiat at the first opportunity and walked back down the boulevard to the agency. There was a sign over the door, in Indonesian and English, that announced: *Tradewinds Travel.*

It did not look like a thriving business. There was a show window that was filthy, with a couple of bent travel displays sitting askew on litter. I went inside and was met with a cool wall of air conditioned air. There was a scarred counter, and a young man behind it. Through an archway, I could see an older fellow working back there, moving boxes of some kind. I leaned on the counter and spoke to the clerk.

'Excuse me. I'm here for Mr Quan.'

The fellow looked up suspiciously, then came over to the counter. 'Mr Quan? Nobody works here by that name, sir.'

He spoke English too well. I always had the most trouble, in foreign places, with clerks who spoke perfect English.

'No,' I said patiently. 'I know he doesn't work here. I came here to pick up his tickets. You remember, he was in the other day.'

He looked me over suspiciously. 'Mr Quan took his ticket with him. There was only one. Why would he send you for a ticket he already has?' There was just a slight touch of arrogant sarcasm in the words.

At least I knew Quan had been there, now. I sighed heavily and reached into my jacket and drew out the Star automatic and showed it to him. His face changed dramatically. His mouth jerked at the corner, and it seemed for a moment he might collapse, he was so afraid of the gun. That was the way I liked it.

'All right, you sonofabitch,' I said bullying him. 'Quan didn't send me. But you just told me he was here, so it's too late to be clever. Where is he going?'

He licked suddenly dry lips, and glanced toward the other room. The older man was not visible now.

'He can't help you,' I said.

His mouth started working. 'He purchased a freighter ticket,' he jerked out nervously. He was a thin fellow with a shock of thick, black hair and pock-marks on his lower face. He was finding it difficult to speak because of the gun. 'To Manila.'

My guess had not been far wrong. 'What company?' I said.

'The Trans-Asian,' was the reply.

'When was he to leave?'

'Tonight. At about nine.'

'What address did he give?'

'He said that if there was any change in departure time, I could call him at a number he gave me.'

'Get the number,' I said.

The clerk fumbled in a file cabinet for a moment, and turned back to me. He had gotten himself slightly under control, but was still very nervous. He read the phone number off to me, watching the Star all the time. I took the paper from him and double-checked the number, and gave it back.

'Thanks,' I said then, stuffing the Star back into my jacket. 'You've been very cooperative.'

Just at that moment, the older man came into the room. He smiled and nodded at me because he thought I was a customer. The clerk became even more nervous with the older man's presence, now that he wanted only for me to leave. I returned the older fellow's nod.

'The service is excellent here,' I said. 'I'll recommend you to all my friends.'

The older fellow smiled widely, but the young man's face blanched slightly. I turned and left.

Back in the new Fiat, I drove to a place where I could call Surabaya at the hospital. I congratulated him on his fast recovery from the gunshot wounds, and he sounded very weak. I asked if all the security was still intact at the hospital, and he assured me that it was. He told me how grateful he was that I had gotten to Colonel Afandi, and how fearful that I should continue on alone. I parried that and requested his cooperation in again running down an address from the phone number I had just acquired. He set the wheels in motion for me. There seemed to be more red tape that time, and it was early afternoon before I got the address from the local phone company. It was a guest house in the northern section of Djakarta.

I drove over there at 2.00, after a light lunch. On the way, I reminded myself that Quan was, politically, the most important of my targets. He had popular support, and that made him very dangerous. He would lose some of that support if his followers knew he had turned killer, but he was a crazy bastard who was capable of reorganization without Afandi and the rest, and starting this secret war up all over again. So Quan was an imperative hit. Machmud and his government would never be safe so long as Quan ran loose in Indonesia.

The guest house was on a shady street in a pleasant neighborhood. It was a large old Dutch colonial house that had been broken up into rooms and small apartments. I parked the Fiat down the street and walked down to the place. There were tall banyan trees in the sizeable yard, and a lot of hibiscus up beside the house. There was no sign of life in the house, but the front door was open, with only a screen door closing off its foyer.

As I stood there, deciding what to do next, a girl came out of the screen door and down the steps toward me, carrying a basket of washing. I figured her for one of the help at the place. I stopped her.

'Which room is Mr Quan's?' I asked, in Indonesian.

'Quan?' she said. She was a thin girl, in her late teens, and she wore a blouse unbuttoned down the front. 'There is no Quan here, *toean*.'

'Perhaps I have the wrong name,' I said. 'The fellow I ask about is a squat, bulky man with black hair. He might have had one or more persons with him. He would have come very recently.'

'Ah! You speak of Mr Toba. Go around to the back, on the main floor. Room number three. I don't know if he is here.'

I nodded and she went on down the walk, on her way to some nearby community washroom, I figured.

I walked around the house. It was quite jungly out back. A bird cried raucously from a big tree. It had the feel of Indonesia bush country back there. I went up three steps and entered the house.

There was a corridor with a musty smell, and room three was on my right, not far from the rear entrance. The house looked deserted. The door of room three, though, stood partially open.

Quan, or somebody, was obviously there.

I drew the Star, wondering whether I was going to get very lucky suddenly. I tapped on the door with the gun. 'Mr Toba?'

There was no reply. I stepped cautiously into the room.

There was an indistinct sound to my right. I started to turn when I saw the big arm come down on my gunhand. It cracked on my wrist like a club.

I yelled out a muffled cry, involuntarily, and then felt myself hit the floor on my side. My ear caught the sound of the Star scraping across a tiled floor, and it was only then that I knew I had lost it.

There was plenty of light in the room, from a shuttered window, so when I turned to get a look at my assailant I saw immediately it was not Quan. The man was square-built and rather tall, obviously one of the two bodyguards Quan had had with him when seen on Djakarta street.

My right wrist radiated pain up into my arm and all through my hand and fingers. At first I thought it was fractured, but it was not. I tried to push myself up with it, and it caved in on me and I hit the floor again. The big man had something in his hand, and when I focused on it, I saw that it was a metal rod over a foot long, with a fancy handle. It was what was popularly called a 'cattle prod' by police in certain parts of the world, an electronic shocking stick that was used against mobs and sometimes in mental institutions and prisons. They were fast being outlawed across the United States because they were very dangerous.

The tough-looking fellow standing over me apparently had purchased his own, or gotten it from Quan. Maybe Quan was stocking up for after his bloody revolution.

I could see a gun bulging the jacket of the big fellow who now stood over me, but the hard grin on his face told me that he felt no necessity to use it. He would rather torture me with the battery-operated prod. I glared up at him, and he motioned for me to get up. He had not spoken a word. He apparently knew exactly who I was, and had waited for this opportunity for quite some time.

I got back up on my knee, watching him carefully. He had positioned himself between me and the Star, which had skittered across the room near a bed. Behind me within a few feet was a wall, so there was no place for me to go. The wrist was giving me fits. I took a deep breath and hurled myself at my opponent.

Halfway there I felt the prod.

It got me in the belly, and I felt an immediate and ugly shock rip through my insides like a hot iron. I grabbed for the big man and missed and fell on my face, doubling up in pain and gasping like a hooked fish. That was what I felt like, too.

I lay there trying to get myself together. The pain had subsided, and I could think of counter-measures again. There was the bed, and a straight chair, and a table with a brass serving tray and empty wine glasses. Nothing in the room that looked like a weapon to me – except for the Star that was out of reach.

I struggled to my knees, and the prod came again. He touched me on the back with it, and I yelled as the voltage jammed through me, ripping me apart inside. I hit the floor again, not able to breathe. I could not take much more, I knew, and have any chance of fighting back. He was slowly killing me. If he prodded me in a vital spot, that would be it.

I lay now beside the table. I saw the big fellow come and kneel beside me, very much in control now, and knowing it.

That was good for me, though – if I could make use of his carelessness.

'Now, Rainey,' he said in Indonesian, hissing it out at me. 'You die slowly and unpleasantly, yes?'

He brought the prod down toward my side, over my left kidney. He was getting serious now. He was going to make me hurt badly – maybe hoping I would plead a little before he killed me. I knew it was all over if I did not think of something fast. He lowered the prod, grinning. I reached up, grabbed the edge of the brass tray on the table, and pulled it off, swinging it in a wide arc toward his face.

The empty glasses crashed to the floor just as the metal tray connected with his fleshy face. There was a loud banging sound as I connected solidly, the brass bending as his face left its impression on it.

The gunman fell heavily onto his back, dropping the prod and grabbing at his face with both hands. I figured at least his nose was busted, and maybe his jaw. He lay there now, groaning between his fingers, probably wondering what had gone wrong – if he was capable of thinking at all. I crawled to the prod, grabbed it, and got to my knees, kneeling beside him. He was yelling more loudly now, and going for the gun in his jacket. I shoved the prod down hard over his heart, and held it there, activating the voltage.

The gunman's eyes flew wide open suddenly, and a croaking sound exploded from his mouth. He forgot the gun and his hands grabbed at the prod convulsively. I shoved hard, keeping it tight against his heart. His body arched violently against it as the voltage ripped through his heart and chest. He could not release the prod now, as his whole torso jumped and jerked with the shock of the voltage.

I deactivated the prod and the gunman's form went limp. His thick hands still held the business end of the weapon he had liked so much, gripping it in rigor mortis now. His eyes stared at the high ceiling, seeing nothing.

He had tortured his last victim.

I got up weakly. I felt like a train had run over me. An anger welled up inside me, and I kicked out viciously at the corpse, hitting it in the side and making it move on the floor. I stood there breathing hard then for a long moment, remembering the ugly prod. I had left it in his grasp, and it stuck up from the center of his chest now, making him look like a vampire that had been killed by driving a stake through his heart.

I went and retrieved the Star and holstered it. The door to the corridor was still open, but there was nobody out there. I looked around the room. There was a phone on a night stand, and no personal belongings of any kind. Quan, crafty to the last, had felt insecure in the room and had left it, probably for good. He had paid this man to stay here through the day, to take any calls about his freighter passage.

That was the way I had it figured, anyway.

My only way to Quan now, I guessed, was to catch him at the freighter before it left at nine p.m.

I was not sorry I had a few hours to kill.

I needed it.

I tried to rest at the hotel when I got back there, but I was keyed high. I had made a call to the freighter line upon my return, and had gotten the name of the freighter that was leaving port at nine. It was the *Celebes*, and it regularly took half a dozen passengers. It was headed for Manila.

It all checked out.

The question was whether the travel agency had called Quan at the guest house before my arrival there. If so, that would account for Quan's absence there, and the fact that the gunman had seemed ready for me.

It would also mean that Quan would go nowhere near the freighter that night. My only hope was that the travel agency people had been too scared of my gun to involve themselves further with Quan, or that if they had called, it was after he left, and the gunman I found there had either not received the call or had not had time to call Quan wherever he was to warn him.

Suddenly it seemed that I was depending on a lot of questionable things to go in my favor.

I forced myself to lie down in the late afternoon, but I could not rest much. At six I got up and cleaned the Star, then paced the floor some more. I spotted Chaban's carrying case in a corner, and went and opened it up. The Belgian Centennial was in there, with its detachable carbine-type stock. There were four silencers, and another automatic, a Luger that was apparently a backup for the Mauser Chaban had always carried with him. It was a formidable array of weaponry. But it had not kept the arrogant Chaban alive.

I wondered what my chances were if I kept on with this.

At 7.37 I left the hotel and went to a small café nearby and had a sandwich and a glass of wine. I did not taste any of it, but I felt I needed it. My body ached all through it, and there was an insistent feeling of fatigue. The electric shocks had taken their toll. It would take me a while to really recover.

It was just after eight when I drove onto the parking area behind the docks, at the waterfront, and parked the car and walked down to the freighter.

It was dark now, but there were lights along the dock. The *Celebes* loomed squat and bulky above me, smelling like oil, with rust running down its massive sides. A foghorn blasted out on the water somewhere. It was a murky night.

I held a small traveling bag in my left hand, filled with scrap cloth. I stood on the dock with it, eyeing the ship's officer at the bottom of the gangplank. Then I took a deep breath and hurried over to him.

I spoke in Indonesian. 'Has Mr Quan boarded?' I asked excitedly.

The officer eyed me diffidently. 'Mr Quan?'

'He was to leave with you tonight. As a passenger.'

The officer raised a clipboard and scanned a sheet on it. 'Ah, yes. I believe Mr Quan boarded just a short time ago.'

'Ah, I thought so. He left this piece of hand luggage behind. May I take it to him? I'll come right back.'

'I can have one of the crew deliver it,' the officer offered.

'Ah, thank you, but I wanted to tell him about some personal articles I added to the case for him.'

He looked me over. 'And your name is – '

'Chaban,' I said. 'I am a business associate of Mr Quan.'

He looked me over again, then nodded. 'All right, Mr Chaban. Be quick about it. We sail presently.'

'Of course,' I said.

I hurried past him up the gangplank. I met a sailor halfway

up, and smiled and crowded past him. Up on the smelly deck, I realized I had not asked which cabin was Quan's. I stopped a white-jacketed steward.

'Which is Mr Quan's cabin?' I asked pleasantly.

'I just settled him in,' the fellow replied. 'Number seven.'

He hurried on past me. I went inside through a low doorway and found an interior walkway. Cabin seven was the third door down the walkway. The door was wide open.

I got a glimpse of Ali Quan inside. He was unpacking a suitcase, and talking to somebody. I figured he had brought a bodyguard with him, the other man of the twosome seen with him outside the travel agency. He had probably booked the fellow a separate cabin.

I set the bag down and looked up and down the corridor. There was nobody about. I had not only to kill Quan, but I had to get off that ship again. I drew the Star and pulled the four-inch silencer from my pocket and screwed it onto the automatic's muzzle. I could hear Quan talking.

'After we get out of port, I will be able to relax,' he was saying quietly. 'I'll cable Rublev from Manila.'

The hell you will, I thought. If I had anything to say about it, Quan's days of wine and roses were behind him. I took a deep breath in. I could not muff this one. It was the most important of all, along with Rublev. I stepped into and through the doorway.

Quan and a tall fellow who looked very much like the one I had killed at the guest house both looked around at me. I felt a deep satisfaction looking eyeball to eyeball with Quan finally.

'Pray, you murdering sonofabitch,' I growled.

Just at that moment, there was a loud blast from the ship's horn, warning those who were not yet aboard that there was a little time. The blast startled me, and I looked away from them for just a moment. The gunman went for the bulge in his jacket.

I swung the Star from Quan to him and fired. The cracking sound of the silenced gun split the stale air, and the tall man was slammed in the high chest and thrown bodily against a bunk beside him, a red stain discoloring his shirt. He hung there for a moment, staring incredulously at the hole in his chest.

Just as I started to swing the gun back to Quan, I heard his voice. 'That will be all, Mr Rainey.'

I turned slightly and looked down the stubby barrel of a .32 revolver. I had not seen him go for it. He must have been carrying it in a side pocket of his suit jacket.

'Now your assassination career is over,' he told me. I saw his finger tighten over the trigger.

I was dead and knew it. But at that precise moment, another interruption broke the chain of events. I saw a sudden movement in the doorway beside me, and the steward was there, the fellow I had just asked about Quan.

'What is going on here?' he said loudly in Indonesian.

As I had before, Quan let his attention wander from me for just a split-second. That tiny instant in time preserved my life and ended Quan's. I fired the silenced Star twice without aiming, hitting Quan in the center chest and face. The second slug entered just beside his broad nose on the right side of his face, and cracked his head audibly on a bunk rail. He threw the revolver spastically across the tiny room and it clanged on a metal wall, then Quan sat on the lower bunk heavily, as if to think over what had just happened to him. A drop of blood wormed out of the hole in his face, and he slowly toppled over backwards onto his back, his eyes and mouth agape.

The steward stood open-mouthed in the doorway. I turned and grabbed him by the shirt with my free hand and hurled him across the cabin. He hit a metal post hard with his back and head, and was stunned. I brought the Star down across his left ear, and he went down like a bag of the Indonesian rice that filled the freighter's hold.

I closed the door quickly, and went to Quan and searched him. I had only moments. In his wallet I found a small paper with a notation scribbled on it in Indonesian. *R by SA* 2315 *HK.*

My head whirled inside. I could hear voices in the corridor. They came to the door and went on past, and disappeared. I breathed again. Stuffing the wallet into my jacket, I went and opened the door carefully. Nobody was out there.

I closed the door behind me and headed for the gangplank. On the way, I thought of the note. If 2315 was a time, meaning 11.15 p.m., and 'R' stood for Rublev, the note could mean that

Rublev was going to do something at that hour. There was a South Asia Airlines that ran regular flights from the local airport, I knew. It was quite probable that Rublev knew Quan was headed out, having been unable to talk him out of it, and decided to leave himself, until things had cooled off. Which meant that we had beaten them. But Quan had been already planning on calling Rublev, before Quan's sudden demise, with the notion, probably, of trying it all again soon, after things had calmed down. I had been right when I decided that the coup could not be considered really dead until both Quan and Rublev were pushing up daisies. That still left Rublev.

Hurrying down the gangplank toward the officer down there, I thought again of the note. 'HK' could stand for Hong Kong, because South Asia flew there regularly. That meant that Rublev would be at the local airport at 11.15, possibly that very evening, to fly away to Hong Kong, then on to Moscow.

I was at the bottom of the gangplank. Some sailors were untying ropes there. I started past the officer who had let me aboard, and he stopped me. 'Excuse me, sir.'

My heart jumped slightly as I turned to him, my hand near the hidden automatic in my jacket. 'Yes?' I said warily.

'Did you find Mr Quan?'

I swallowed hard. 'Oh. Yes, I did. He was pleased to get his bag.'

He nodded. 'You are very lucky. We are just now raising the gangplank.'

'Yes,' I nodded. 'Very lucky indeed.'

A moment later I was halfway across the dock, heading for the Fiat.

My time, and hopefully Rublev's, was running out fast.

Twelve

From the moment I had learned of Rublev's involvement in the assassination plot, I knew he was the ultimate target. It was Rublev who had sneaked into Indonesia from his KGB lair in Moscow to suggest multiple murder to the PLA five. It was Rublev, too, who had undoubtedly masterminded the whole coup attempt, and supplied the funds and know-how to Quan and his cohorts that they sorely needed. Rublev was leaving now, I knew, only because he had momentarily run out of allies. If I let him leave, he would be back – next month, or next year. Mokri Dela did not give up. They were always there, waiting.

But if Rublev did not come back, they would have something to think about. Men like Rublev were hard to develop. When they lost one like him, they had lost something.

I thought of all that as my Fiat roared along the boulevard toward the airport. The note, I knew, was not all that specific. There was no date, unless it was in code. That meant that Rublev might have left last evening, or intended to fly away two or three days from now. But the most likely conclusion was that Quan had made the note earlier that day, and did not mention a date because it was the same day Quan himself was leaving.

It was a long ride to the airport from the docks, and when I got there and had debarked from the Fiat, it was 10.27.

There was a lot of traffic at the airport. I made my way through a small crowd near the doors and went directly to the reservation counter for South Asia Airlines. A short Indonesian girl in a blue uniform greeted me there.

'May I help you?' she said in English.

'A friend of mine is leaving on your flight 306 tonight, at 11.45,' I said. 'His name is Vasil Rublev. Has he been here at the desk yet?'

'Rublev,' she mused, thinking. 'I don't recall that name, sir.'

'Can you check to make sure he's on the passenger manifest?' I said to her.

She shook her head. 'That is against the law, sir. I can't reveal the names of any passengers.'

I had known so, but thought it was worth a try. I thanked her, and walked slowly down the way, along the other desks. If Rublev's reservation was for another night, I was wasting my time. I found Concourse C, the one that South Asia flight 306 left from, and walked down the concourse until I came to the proper gate. There were chairs in a waiting lounge, and a few people had gathered there, but none of them were Rublev.

I suddenly felt very weary. I leaned against the concourse wall, thinking. If Rublev was booked on this flight, he would probably be there by now. Unless he had seen me out at the reservation area and I had scared him off.

That was very likely, I knew.

It was probable that somehow I had blown it.

Suddenly the success against Quan and the others did not seem like such a great victory. Without Rublev, it all seemed incomplete. Wasted effort, to a certain degree.

I checked out the men's room in the concourse and came up empty, and then went through the same thing out in the main part of the terminal. I walked up and down the length of the terminal, and ended up back at the South Asia desk. Again, the girl had not seen a Mr Rublev. I figured he must be using an alias, anyway, so I described him to her. She got cagey and said she did not remember. She was becoming suspicious of me.

It was 11.00, and they were calling the flight on the loudspeaker. Something had gone wrong, I knew it. I would go down to the boarding gate again, wait until everybody had boarded, and then give it up. I would have to call Machmud and tell him I had gotten Quan, but might have allowed Rublev to slip through our fingers.

It was not going to be a pleasant thing to do.

I was just about to turn and head back down to Concourse C, when I glanced down the terminal and saw him.

It was Rublev. He had just stopped dead in his tracks, and was staring hard at me. He was a hundred yards away, and there were a few people milling between us, but each of us recognized the other immediately.

I saw Rublev's face settle into a dark scowl. He had absolutely no fear of me, I knew. But he did not want and could not afford a violent confrontation in the air terminal. As for me, I had formulated no definite plan of action for a confrontation. I knew only that I had to kill him. An arrest was not sufficient, any more than it had been for Quan and the others.

He set his small bag down carefully near a reservation desk, gave me an ugly look, and turned and headed back down the other way.

I took off after him, walking rapidly. The Star was wearing its silencer under my jacket, but it was too soon to draw it. I wondered if Rublev was armed. He could not get aboard the plane with a gun, and he had already abandoned his overnight bag. I walked quickly past it without stopping, trying to close the distance between me and Rublev.

Rublev glanced over his shoulder and saw me coming, and broke into a run. I began running, too, drawing the Star now. Rublev ran into a woman, knocked her down and kept on going. She and another woman screamed when they saw my gun. I raced past them on down to the end of the terminal, where Rublev was leaving the building by a service door.

I stopped fifty yards away and aimed the Star with both hands grasping it firmly, just as Rublev was going through the door. I fired and the muffled Star cracked out above the terminal noise and the slug missed Rublev by inches, caroming off the metal door beside him.

A man near me yelled at me, and then suddenly I felt him hit me, knocking the Star down and throwing his other arm around my neck. I had run into a citizen hero.

Rublev was out of sight now. I threw an elbow into the ribs of the traveler – he looked like an American or Briton – and he grunted hard and fell off me. I turned and jammed stiffened fingers into his throat, and he croaked out an ugly sound and fell onto his side, gurgling and making odd sounds.

There was more screaming from down the way. I ignored it and ran on down to the door to the outside, and went through it. Rublev was nowhere in sight.

I was standing on a concrete apron between the terminal and a nearby hangar, with a fence between me and the public parking lot beyond it. I looked at the lot, and the hangar building, and made my choice. I headed for the hangar. Just as I rounded the corner of it, I saw Rublev disappear inside big hangar doors.

I ran down to the big entrance, and saw a two-engine Cessna warming up just inside. Two men were on the far side of the plane, and one was Rublev. He had just handed the other fellow, who apparently was the pilot, a wad of money, and now Rublev was getting aboard the small craft. I ran to the plane as the pilot followed him aboard.

'Hey!' I yelled to the man. *'Stop right there!'*

He either did not see my gun, or felt he was too committed to turn back. He was in the plane now, getting into the pilot's seat. Rublev had ducked low, and I could not see him. The pilot gunned the engine and headed right for me, through the doors.

I aimed quickly and fired, to wound him, but the plane jerked slightly and the slug only spidered the windshield. The right prop was coming right at my head. If it connected, I would be decapitated in style. I dived for the ground, and a wheel brushed my arm as the plane rolled past, making a tornado wind around me, its engines drowning out all other sound.

I waited until it had passed, then turned and got on one knee and aimed carefully after it. It was taxiing fast now, leaving the hangar. I aimed at the fuel tank just behind the engine and fired three quick shots off. On the second shot, there was a small yellow explosion behind the engine, and then a lot of flame as the plane caught fire.

Almost immediately the Cessna began taxiing in a tight circle, then stopped near the hangar as the pilot came falling out the open door. He hit the concrete hard, and hurt himself, and did not get up. Rublev came diving out next, with his back aflame. He rolled on the concrete and put it out.

I went over closer to him as he turned onto his side, toward me, gasping shallowly. I wanted to make sure when I squeezed that trigger for the last time. But when I got there, Rublev suddenly pulled his right hand up toward me and there was something in it.

'Hold it, Rainey!' he growled.

He was aiming a cannister gun at me, one of those gas guns that fire a dart loaded with deadly and fast-acting poison.

'It's all tough new plastic,' he explained, a hard grin on his face, *'and is undetectable at the airport check. The only metal is a very thin needle, one that cannot be picked up by their machines, Rainey, but which will kill you in thirty seconds. Sorry about that. You'll still take me with you, but at least I'll have the satisfaction of killing you first.'*

His face was all twisted up in hatred as he lay there on his side. Smoke still rose from his burned back, and he looked as if his left leg might be busted, the way it was bent under him. The Cessna's engines roared near us, and Rublev had had to yell to make me hear him. But his face told me it was worth it to him, to explain his cleverness to me.

I had no time to avoid his shot. There was a sharp popping sound from the gas gun, and simultaneously a tiny dart hit me just to the left of my heart, over the aorta. Rublev's strained grin widened.

For an instant I thought I was a dead man. But then I realized that the dart had not punctured my flesh under the suit jacket. I felt the place, and my hand found the wallet of Ali Quan, that I had stuffed into my breast pocket in the freighter cabin. The dart had hit it, and the thick wallet had saved my life.

I carefully removed the dart, avoiding its poison tip, and threw it at my feet. Rublev's face changed, and he was staring at me as if I had performed some incredible feat of magic.

'It hit Quan's wallet,' I yelled above the engines, making my own little smug explanation now. I had raised the Star, and it was aimed at Rublev's chest. *'A millimeter to the right and you'd have made it. But now you'll have to go alone.'*

I squeezed the trigger, and the Star could hardly be heard above the roar of the engines. Rublev jumped on the concrete like a spastic cripple, and hit on his back with his arms flung wide. His eyes stared into the black sky, but were glazing over quickly. His outflung right arm slapped the pavement once and that was the end of it.

The Indonesian conspiracy was over.

For good.

The pilot lay half-conscious ten yards away, but a small

crowd of gathering people had now gathered down by the terminal building. I holstered the Star quickly and hurried through the hangar to a service door at its far end. In just moments I was in the parking lot again, and gunning the engine of the Fiat. I had just cleared the airport gate when I heard the blare of police klaxons down the road.

They were too late.

On the way to my flea-bag hotel I stopped and called Machmud. He was stunned to learn that it was over. He could not seem to believe it. I felt the same way. He would call Surabaya immediately, and give him the good news. He was going to declare a special holiday for all of Indonesia. He would go on the radio and give a long speech, telling the people how important it was to rally behind their government. Without admitting anything, he would hint that Quan and the others had been foreign-influenced enemies of the state. It would be a long time before anybody tried to walk in Quan's rebellious footsteps in Indonesia.

Machmud wanted to give me another bonus, and I declined. All I wanted now, I told him, was rest. He said he understood. I doubted it.

When I hung up, I made a second call. This one was a spur-of-the-moment call to Nellie Ullah. Her voice was music to my ears.

'Jim! What a nice surprise!'

'Are you busy?' I asked.

'I was just on my way to bed.'

'That makes it even nicer,' I told her.

I heard her laugh softly. 'You're coming over, then?'

'I can't bring myself to return to that bake-oven room of mine where the roaches are about to begin their nightly soccer game on my bed,' I said.

'Does that mean you'll stay all night?'

'I might be there a week,' I suggested.

'You mean it's over?'

'It's over, Nellie.' I saw Rublev's twisted body again, in my head, jumping on the pavement as the Star's slug hit him. The memory gave me considerable satisfaction.

'I'll see you shortly, then?' Nellie was asking me.

The airport scene dissolved like a morning fog burned off by the sun, and was replaced by a lovely vision of Nellie in a brief nightie, with all those incredible curves shaping and molding it to her, and her aroma, sweet and musky, and I remembered how soft she was to touch and to hold.

'I'll run all the way,' I said.